A Cowboy for Christmas

Serendipity, Indiana - Book Nine

by

Magdalena Scott

A Cowboy for Christmas

© 2017 Magdalena Scott

ISBN-13: 978-0-9971922-9-2

Edited by Karen Block

Cover Art by Elusive Dreams Designs
Stock Art from DepositPhotos.com

Published by Jewel Box Books

Acknowledgments

A big shout-out to the folks on my newsletter list who
submitted names
for Michael Hollingsworth's horse:
Jennifer Butry
Judy Flynn
Teresa Fordice
Linda D. McKnight
Helen Mudd
Kathleen O'Donnell
Oakley R.
Dorothy Roller
Sheila Schwartz
Susan Shields
Carol Smith
Robin Weiss
Charlene Whitehouse
Caroline Woodhall
Xgamer

A COWBOY FOR CHRISTMAS

Chapter One

HIS EYES WERE wild with hatred. His breath escaped in hot, fast gasps. Everyone had told me that coming here was a mistake, and they were about to be proven very right. Unable to move, I watched as he leaned down. At the last second, I closed my eyes…

A soft, warm sensation tickled my outstretched palm. Then silence.

Opening my eyes, I met his for a moment before he tossed his head and snorted at my obvious fear. I had survived for now, but wondered what would happen next time.

My friend Jessica nudged me. "Hannah. Chill out, girlfriend. You lived through it."

I sucked in a deep breath and stepped back from the massive chestnut horse on the other side of the wood slat fence. Killer—what an apt name. Turning, I managed a weak smile at Jessica. "Wow. You were right. That wasn't so bad."

She laughed loudly. "You passed apple slice administration 101, but just barely. It couldn't be more obvious you're afraid of horses. Tell me again why you wanted to work here on the Rocking H. Be sure to include the part that it has nothing to do with my brother Jacob." When she mentioned his name, her face clouded, but in an instant was back to normal.

We'd had this conversation before, she and her sister Ashley and I, over coffee by the massive native-stone fireplace in the chuck wagon building. Now, Jessica and I walked away from the corral toward the dude ranch's chuck wagon and guest housing. A cold wind blew my hair into my face. I pulled a scrunchie out of my jeans pocket, ran my fingers through my red hair, and created a thick ponytail. These days, looking good was reserved for evenings out, and there were few of those. How far I'd fallen since the days at Indiana University-Bloomington, when I didn't leave the dorm floor looking less than my best.

"I'm still waiting for a job in environmental management," I said. "I have profiles posted everywhere I can think of, and every night I follow up on whatever I find online. But in Serendipity, this is the closest thing to it."

"Closest thing to a job or to environmental management?" She waved a hand, not expecting a response. "I know, I know. Ashley and I adore having you here while you try to find the right position to start your career. But we're afraid that, even temporarily, it's not a good fit for you."

"I'll get used to the horses. I'm making progress already, don't you think?"

She was silent, but her facial expression spoke volumes.

"Okaa-ay. I *will* make progress. I've only been here a month, after all. I appreciate the two of you hiring me when the tree farm job ended. Especially since you sort of went behind your brothers' backs to do it."

"Jacob's fine. He has plenty to take care of and keep his mind busy without second-guessing our staffing choice. And Michael—well, he doesn't know what's happening here except very generally."

As far as I could tell, he didn't care either. Three siblings lived and worked at the ranch—Jessica, Ashley, and Jacob. Michael, whom I'd never met, seemed to be a partner in name only. The fact that Killer, Michael's horse, lived here seemed to indicate he had an intention of visiting sometime. Either that or he had abandoned the horse, just as it seemed he had abandoned his siblings.

The Rocking H Dude Ranch had opened just six months ago and had done better than most folks in Serendipity expected. For a small backward town, we had some outside-the-box businesses, like the bed and breakfast added to the Standish family's Christmas tree farm across the road from the Rocking H. B&B guests stayed in tiny cabins sprinkled among the acres of Christmas trees. The location of Serendipity, twenty miles from the nearest interstate, had kept the town from growing as much as some of the other county seats, so recent improvements had been needed.

Jessica picked up her pace. "Come on. We have

work to do."

"Whatever I need to do today is an easy downhill slide from having my palm investigated by Killer's mouth."

"Muzzle," she corrected, giggling. "And you're probably right about that."

We cleaned and straightened guest rooms while their occupants were on a trail ride with Jacob and Ashley. Twenty guests—a full complement, in spite of the chill November weather. When the guest rooms were finished, Jessica started dinner, and I cleaned the rest of the building interior. This day, like every day since graduating from IU in the spring, was light years away from what I envisioned.

Everyone returned mid-afternoon. After seeing to the horses with help from Jacob, Ashley, and Jessica, the guests burst into the chuck wagon laughing and cheerfully complaining of soreness. I served hot cocoa and soft drinks while the people who knew all things dude ranch finished up in the barn. Much of what happened here was beyond the scope of my position.

When the siblings entered the room full of

guests, there was an obvious rise in enthusiasm. Every set of visitors relished the experience of playing cowboy for a few days while staying at the rustic dude ranch. Jacob's handsome face was glowing with his enjoyment of the way he spent his work days.

When I handed him a cup of cocoa, he thanked me and put an arm around my shoulders. "Having you here with us on the Rocking H makes everything better, Hannah."

Part of my reason for seeking this temporary job was to get to know Jacob, but so far that hadn't worked out as planned. When we were together, he was funny, engaging, and flirtatious. But he was the same way with everyone else. I had fallen for him on sight, but months into our "relationship," I was still nothing special to Jacob Hollingsworth.

The first time I met him was this summer when I was working at the Christmas tree farm. As new neighbors, he, Jessica, and Ashley paid a visit. He was tall and slim, in well-worn jeans and a pale blue Western shirt that matched his eyes. His tan was deep, and his Stetson white. To me, he was a perfect specimen of what a cowboy should look like. He even called my boss, Francie Standish Carrington, *ma'am*, which I thought was very brave. My mom feels old when people call her that, but I couldn't tell what Francie thought about it.

It's possible that Jacob's sparkling eyes and brilliant smile helped soften the blow. They sure did things to me.

Now, one of the guests asked him a question. He crossed the room, squatted down next to her, and soon had everyone in the palm of his hand with his easy repartee and folksy stories.

I realized what I was doing wrong here. Being the support staff would never bring me close to Jacob. I needed to be part of the important goings-on of the ranch. My stomach clutched. That meant doing more than timidly feeding apple slices to horses. I needed to learn to ride.

Chapter Two

SINCE MY TWIN sister Taylor's marriage, our relationship had evolved. I was happy for her but struggled with the loss of the near-constant companionship we'd had since birth. We had set aside Thursday evening each week as Twin Time and, so far, had a perfect record. I had to be satisfied with three or four hours together, because by the end of that period, she was always eager to get home to Ken. Or if he was out too, there was some discreet texting about when they'd return to their apartment on the third story of Once Upon a Time, the antiques store they owned. Tonight Taylor and I would meet at the Barbeque Basement.

I drove into town from Mom and Dad's house in

the Ford Focus the two of us used to share. Eager for our evening, I had arrived a bit early.

The restaurant does a great job with its simple menu and good service, but a big part of its charm is the ambiance. I walked down the dark stairway and opened the heavy wooden door into the huge rock-and-brick-walled basement. The white, heavily textured ceiling always reminded me of stalactites. The floor was concrete and brick, and there was a rough wood bar along the left wall. The tables and chairs were sturdy but certainly not fancy.

On weekend nights the place was full to overflowing, but on Thursdays, you could actually engage in a conversation without shouting over the din of music and surrounding diners whose voices were also raised to be heard. I enjoyed raucous evenings and always had, but Twin Time was different.

Hank Blandings, the owner, greeted me. "Hey, Hannah. How's it goin'?"

A few months ago, it would have been, *Hannah? Or is it Taylor?* To most people we looked identical. In fact, talking to Taylor sometimes felt like talking into a mirror. Yet I had always considered her the pretty one—blue eyes set in a creamy complexion perfectly framed by red hair. Depending on the effort put forth, the thick locks might show their natural wave, or cascade in a sleek, flat-ironed line.

Now that my sister was married, it just took a quick glance at our left hands for anyone to know which twin was which. The days of pulling one over on our teachers or casual acquaintances were gone. Another piece of the past fading into history.

"I'm good, Hank. How about a two-top? I'm meeting Taylor."

Hank picked up menus and gestured at the nearly empty room. "Wide selection of possibilities right now. How about the far corner so you girls can visit without anybody bothering you?"

"Works for me."

I followed him to the corner by the stage which wouldn't be used tonight. It also put us away from the juke box, thank goodness. Taylor would pop in soon, having walked over from Once Upon a Time. The antiques store was on the Serendipity town square, which surrounded our castle-like courthouse.

When we were growing up, back-to-school shopping was done at the shoe and clothing store above this basement area. The two-story establishment boasted an impressive inventory of sensible shoes, shirts, and Levi jeans. The upstairs now housed an upscale children's shop, and the basement-turned-restaurant was a relatively new and surprisingly successful addition to town. Anything with less than twenty-five years of history was *new* in Serendipity.

The restaurant entrance down some rough stone steps on the north end of the building faced an insufficient parking lot and a small apartment block on West Walnut Street. If there'd been a window in the south end of the space, it would have looked out on the courthouse. Or, more accurately, the sidewalk in front of the children's shop and next door to The Jewelry Box.

As usual, the Basement was dimly lit and permeated with the mouth-watering smell of slow-cooked meat.

"What are you ladies drinking tonight,

Hannah?"

"Let's start with two glasses of ice water with lemon, Hank. What do you have on draft?"

From memory, he gave me the run-down of a dozen choices, and I picked a lager for myself.

Once a week I had a beer. I was still trying to save money, because if I found a job I wanted, I'd need cash on hand to relocate to *wherever* and get a place to live. But back in our carefree college days, we sure didn't limit ourselves to one beer when we went out on weekends in Bloomington. Those were the good old days, at least for me.

While Hank spoke to the bartender, I tried to quash my impatience to see Taylor and start our weekly reconnect. I was eager to tell her about my decision to become more involved at the dude ranch. I sort of wanted her input on the idea, but if she didn't like it, I'd just do what I thought best. She'd certainly done her own thing and ended up with Ken.

Bouncing my crossed leg with typical nervous energy, I did a surreptitious scan of the diners. Only a couple of other tables were occupied. At the first sat two older couples, probably Gran's age. At the other was The Jewelry Box owner and his wife. I waved at them and they waved back. Pretty handy to walk out the back door of their shop at quitting time and have dinner here.

The menu, a sheet of paper printed on just one side and encased in heavy plastic, lay in front of me, but I knew I would order the brisket platter. My life had become boring and predictable, so typical of living in a small town.

Finally, Taylor blew in the door, her smile wide as she gave Hank a quick hug and spoke for a moment. "Yeah, I see her," she said, and greeted everyone else on her way to join me.

I hopped up, and we hugged. "Hey, I thought you'd never get here."

She sat down and dropped her big handbag onto the floor next to her. "I know. I'm sorry. We had a customer who wanted to chat a little long. Can't just shove people out the door, you know. It's bad for business."

When she first started working at the antiques

store, she didn't have that outlook. Taylor had changed a lot in just a few months. It was a shock to see her fitting so well into small town life, after all the time we'd spent complaining about it. Her smile wouldn't stop, and her skin and eyes glowed. "You're looking awesome," I said.

"Thanks. So are you."

"No, I'm not. I did manage a shower and makeup for this evening though. That's a big deal these days."

Hank brought the drinks, and Taylor said she was fine with water. We both ordered the brisket dinner, and he went away into the kitchen.

"Must be short staffed tonight," I said.

"I imagine he tries to save money on labor when he can. Small business, you know."

I took a sip of my beer. "Yeah. Speaking of small business, I've just realized what I've been doing wrong at the Rocking H."

"Oh? And what's that—looking desperate?"

"I haven't been looking desperate. Just…interested." I sipped again. "No, what I need to do is start helping with the trail rides and the horses and stuff."

Taylor shook her head. "Hannah. You're afraid of large dogs. I don't see you riding horses. Have you managed to get on one of them?"

It was so weird and unfair that I had this fear and Taylor did not. "Well, no. But I gave an apple slice to Killer today."

Taylor had been to the ranch a few times. Ashley and Jessica and the two of us managed, once in a great while, to do a shopping trip or an evening together at the ranch between guests. "Hmm. Feeding Killer an apple slice is big. If you're comfortable with him, you've made more progress than I realized."

I fiddled with the thick cardboard drink coaster. "To be honest, he and I aren't exactly buddies. But I'm going to keep working on it plus spending time with the other horses and helping in the barn and whatever."

"Honey, you don't even know what you're talking about. Have you discussed this idea with Jessica and Ashley? And Jacob?"

I wasn't a child in need of a lecture. "I know

manure is involved, Taylor, if that's what you're saying. And no, I haven't brought it up with them yet. But I will. Tomorrow."

She nodded. "If you're sure." She paused, lowered her voice. "Just—maybe Jacob isn't—" Her eyes grew wide, and I followed her gaze. Jacob had just come in the door, and with him was another cowboy.

Wait. Two tall, tanned, handsome cowboys in the Barbeque Basement on a Thursday night? Life just got weirder and weirder.

Jacob saw us, smiled, and waved. He spoke to his companion and gestured toward us. The other man nodded, and Jacob led the way across the room. I met Taylor's eyes. She looked about ready to pop out of her seat. She turned away from them and whispered, "Oh boy, I'm glad I'm married to the most wonderful man in the world, because, otherwise, I'd be tempted."

Jacob was smiling in his usual, light-up-the-room way. "Hey there. This is some great timing, huh?" He looked up at the other guy. Hard to believe he had to look *up*, because Jacob was over six feet tall. But his friend wasn't smiling in return.

"You going to do some introductions, little brother?" the stranger asked.

Brother? I should have noticed the resemblance before. Dark hair, blue eyes, Roman nose. The brother looked a few years older.

Jacob nodded. "This is Hannah. Remember, Michael, we told you about her. And her sister, Taylor."

Michael did what Taylor and I refer to as the Twin Double-Take. "Nice to meet you, ladies."

While my voice was caught in my throat, Taylor spoke up. "It's nice to meet you, Michael. Please excuse my surprise. For some reason, I had the idea there were just three siblings in the Hollingsworth family."

"They probably try to *pretend* I don't exist, but, stubbornly, I do." The barest hint of a smile briefly tugged at a corner of his chiseled mouth.

Jacob huffed out a breath. "We don't do anything of the sort. The three of us came here to start the dude ranch. Michael was—doing other things. Mom and Dad live in a retirement community in Florida, if we haven't already told you that."

That information had been shared early on. Parents retired, selling their small ranch in Montana. The kids went their own ways for a few years, then decided that opening a dude ranch in a more accessible and winter-weather friendly part of the country than their home state of Montana was the ideal joint project for the three of them. I looked hard at each man in turn. Michael had been mentioned a couple of times, but why hadn't anyone told me he was coming for a visit?

We managed a little more small talk, but Michael was clearly ready to end the conversation. "You ladies have a nice evening." He gestured to us with the white Stetson he'd taken off when they entered. He shot Jacob a meaningful look before leading the way to the bar, where they sat down and began to talk in low tones.

Watching them, Taylor smiled, her eyes sparkling. "Well. That's interesting. The arrival of the secret brother. What do you make of it, Hannah?"

I shrugged. "I don't know. It's nothing to me." But it bothered me that, for whatever reason, I'd been left out of the Rocking H information loop.

My sister crossed her arms. "Come on, Michael is interesting. I bet he has quite a story. I wonder if he's coming here to live or just passing through."

The guys had neatly sidestepped Taylor's inquisitive questions. It made no sense to be so secretive, unless Michael had a sordid past. "Maybe he has a criminal record. He looks a little shifty to me."

She fanned herself in mock hot-flash. "Do you think so? I think he's gorgeous. I'll be sure to describe him in great detail to Ken when I get home." She put down her hand. "You're certainly playing it cool."

"I'm not interested in anyone but Jacob."

"Hmm. I wish he appeared to return your feelings. But remember, he's settled here, and you're looking for a way out of Serendipity."

That part was tricky, but I refused to waste time on reasons *not* to be interested in Jacob. "Don't judge so quickly."

She started to say something but shut her mouth again. "Okay. What you do in your love life and your job is your call. You know I only want whatever's best for you, right?"

I sipped from my mug again but the flavor was soured by the turn of events this evening. "Yes. I know you're looking out for me. But remember, Taylor, we're all grown up. We get to make our own choices. I didn't try to talk you out of loving Ken."

"True. I won't point out the fact that the relationship between Ken and me was, and is, completely different from your dude ranch romance."

Meaning Taylor had been working at the shop for a while before the love bug bit, and when it did, they were both receptive. Not, in other words, like me chasing Jacob. "Good. Thanks for not pointing that out. Can we talk about something else?"

We did, catching up on local gossip, "new" items that had come into the antiques store this week, and the continued success of the tea room and weekend dining nooks set into the shop windows. I was glad the dining was making enough money that Taylor hired a local woman to help out. I no longer had to volunteer to run the kitchen or serve tables. By the end of a week at my own job, I looked forward to spending my free time on the couch in front of the TV or in my room online.

I wondered if this was what it felt like to be old. Mom and Dad went out together at least once a week and were hardly home at all on weekends. They saw plays, visited museums, and attended music festivals. For that matter, our grandmother had more of a social life than I did.

I slid a glance to the Hollingsworth brothers again. They were both smiling, still talking softly.

"I know," Taylor said, interrupting my thoughts. "I'm dying to hear what they're saying too. Maybe you'll learn more tomorrow at the dude ranch. Jacob, Jessica, and Ashley can't very well hide him away completely."

An idea occurred to me. "Hey, his showing up might be just what I need. If he's here to work on the ranch, it will take some of the pressure off Jacob to always be chatting up the guests and leading trail rides."

I could imagine it. Jacob and I taking long walks, holding hands, discussing all the things we had in common and what we wanted out of life. "Yeah. I'm thinking the unexpected appearance of Michael will make a real difference in my future with Jacob."

Taylor sipped her water, not meeting my eyes. When she set down her glass, she took a moment before replying. "I think you might be right about that. Michael could make all the difference in the world."

Chapter Three

I WAS A little bit late to work the next day. Never an early riser, the seven o'clock start time was a daily challenge. Being tired didn't help. I had spent much of the night tossing and turning, as my mind presented dozens of possible scenes for my new role on the ranch and in Jacob's life.

I parked in my usual spot and hurried into the chuck wagon. A fire crackled in the great room fireplace and the tables were laid for breakfast. Ashley and Jessica had the meal going, which was a relief. At least, nothing was off schedule because I'd slept through my alarm.

I pulled on an apron. "Hey, guys. Sorry I'm late. Crazy night."

"Is that right?" The deep voice surprised me, and when I turned around, Michael filled the entire doorway to the dining room.

My wits seemed to leave me. An appropriate response wouldn't form itself. "Umm. Overslept."

His frown was directed at me. "Breakfast is under control, as you can see. I've been told that you *work* here, Hannah. If that's the case, since Ashley is pulling your breakfast shift, you can fill in for her."

"But..." Ashley's eyes, suddenly wild, went from him to me. She set down the potato she was peeling and tugged at the tie of her apron. "I'll just go now, and let Hannah take over for me. It's better that way."

He glowered at her. "The ranch will be most efficient if everybody is cross-trained to do all the jobs, wouldn't you agree?" He looked to me, and I might have nodded, following the motion of his head.

"Where's Jacob?" I asked.

Michael's frown deepened. "That's no concern of yours. He was up and moving early, in spite of our visit to the same bar you seem to frequent. If you can't hold your liquor, you'd better leave drinking to the times you don't have to be at work the next day."

My face heated with anger. "How dare you judge my reason for being late or anything else about me?"

"I dare because I help pay your wages, Ms. Kincaid." He took a step back and gestured toward the doorway he'd left partly open. "Now let's head to the barn and get the horses ready for their day."

Jessica stepped to him and put a hand on his arm. "Michael, come on. Please let Hannah help me. She's a much better cook than Ashley is." Ashley shot her a look. They were both trying to save me from being found out as horse-challenged.

Michael scanned his sisters' faces. "If that's the case, Ashley needs to hone her cooking skills. Shame on you, little sister," he scolded her. "I remember the two of you preparing some pretty terrific meals back when we all lived at home to give Mom the night off. Jess, are you telling me that Ashley didn't pull her weight back then, and you covered up for her?"

They both cringed, caught in a lie either way.

Without knowing Michael at all, I was certain he would have a dim view of lying. And they were only in this position because they were trying to protect me.

"Come on, Michael," I said. "We don't have all morning." I walked past him—no small feat because his broad shoulders still partly filled the doorway. He smelled of a musky after-shave and wood smoke. He must have been the one who started the fire this morning. If the aroma combination had been on Jacob, I would have found it entrancing. But on Michael, it was just annoying, like him.

Once we exited the building and walked toward the barn, I had to hurry to keep up with his much longer stride.

"Where did you come from, anyway?" I asked.

He didn't spare me a glance, just kept his eyes forward. "Ms. Kincaid, you look very young, but surely your parents have explained to you about the birds and the bees. That knowledge is important, if you and your sister are in the habit of late nights at the local bars."

Fine. He wanted to poke at me? I was in a bear of a mood and glad to poke back. "Ha. You are cracking me up with that dry wit of yours, Mr. Hollingsworth. You know what I mean. Your brother and sisters have been here for months, getting the existing buildings converted and the chuck wagon and bunk house built. They've worked really hard to get the dude ranch started, and make it a success. Yet now, after all the work is done, you pop up and start making trouble. Why? And *yes*, where did you come from?"

We had stopped in the middle of the gravel parking area just outside the barn. Facing each other, hands on hips, I hoped none of the guests would look out their windows and see me in this confrontational posture. I buttoned my heavy coat, wishing for a warm hat. Thinking I was going to work in the kitchen, I'd pulled my hair straight back into a ponytail before leaving home. My ears were already freezing.

Michael pinned me with a steely gaze, slightly shaded by the brim of his Stetson. "Let me make this simple for you. My presence here is none of your business, except that you now have a *boss* and not just three buddies. As far as I have been able to discern, you show up when you feel like it, do a few tasks here and there, and at the end of the week, get a paycheck. That version of your responsibilities ends today. Understand?" He turned on his heel and opened the barn door, and paused there, as if waiting for me to precede him. It reminded me of the ultimatum from Dad when Taylor and I finished college and, with no jobs in our fields, moved back home.

"Yeah, I understand," I muttered. Now I knew why nobody had mentioned him before. They were probably hoping he wouldn't show up and ruin everything they had going for them. I could imagine Michael's horrible disposition would scare guests away and ensure the positive word-of-mouth advertising took a terrible turn to the negative.

What a shame. I hoped he could feel the disdain rolling off me as I stepped into the barn, ignoring his musk-and-wood-smoke aroma as I was met by a different one entirely.

Horse …stuff. Oh boy.

An eternity later, I pushed the last wheelbarrow load and dumped it. Until this morning, I had a general idea the horse manure was recycled into fertilizer to be spread on crops. The general idea had been much more pleasant than the reality. Now I knew exactly how much it stunk, how much a shovel-full weighed, and—well—how much it stunk.

I couldn't even go to the chuck wagon for a drink of water, because if I did, I would smell up the entire building. Halfway through the task, Michael brought me a jug of water and an aluminum cup. I didn't drink out of it when he could see me, but when he disappeared, I gulped it down. Every muscle in my body screamed at me for abusing them.

When all but one of the stalls was mucked out and had fresh straw on the floor, I hesitated, catching my breath. Killer was still in residence, though all the other horses had been turned into the corral in preparation for today's ride. I stood there watching him, and he eyed me with the hatred I had grown to expect. No way was I going to risk cleaning his stall with him in there. That was even crazier than trying to get a halter and rope on him, to lead him down the aisle to the corral. Michael could verbally abuse me all he wanted, but I wasn't going to touch that horse. I valued my life too much.

The barn door opened with a long squeak, and I turned, expecting to see my tormentor. But it was Jacob. I'd never been so happy to see him, and that's saying a lot. I started to walk toward him before remembering what I must smell like.

A slow smile lit his handsome face. "Hey, Hannah. Michael told me you were in here. How's it going?" I guess he caught a whiff, because he cringed for a moment. "Wow. Gotta love the behind-the-scenes work of the ranch, right? Is this your first time cleaning stalls? Michael said you didn't seem to know one end of a pitchfork from the other."

I knew which end I'd like to apply to his older brother's posterior. "I'll bet he said that and probably worse."

Jacob's face reddened. "Michael is hard to get to know. Just give him time."

So he was taking up for his brother, in spite of what I was being put through. I shrugged, hoping to appear disinterested in the whole matter. I *was* disinterested in Michael, but how could Jacob ignore his brother's treatment of me? And how in the world could Jacob not realize this was my first time cleaning stalls? Was I *that* invisible to him?

"How much time?" I asked. "I mean, how long is he going to visit?"

"It's not exactly a visit, Hannah. Michael is part owner, you know."

"Of course, I didn't know. How would I? Not that it's any of my business, but even as an employee..." I took a breath, not wanting my words to sound like a rant. "Why in the world did none of you ever warn—I mean—tell me anything about him? I mean, he just shows up, and starts giving orders like he owns the place."

Jacob smiled. "He's family, he *is* part owner, and we are all used to the way he comes across. You caught him at a bad moment."

My heart was thumping, but not the way it usually did when Jacob was around. I was angry. "The *bad moment* started last night when I met this phantom brother of yours at the Basement, has continued through an awkward scene in the kitchen, and through a million trips with a wheel barrow load of manure. At some point, is he going to suddenly become human?"

Sheepish, Jacob slid his hands into his pockets. The door closed with a bang, and there was Michael.

"No, I'm not going to become human. If that's a problem for you, Hannah, I can write a check for what the ranch owes you, and we'll all say farewell."

I put my hands on my hips—it seemed the way I always stood when interacting with Michael—trying to stare him down. "I wouldn't quit and give you the satisfaction. This is my job, and I'm staying until I find something better. Though since your arrival, something better is pretty much anything in the world."

That was a lie. If I left, I'd lose my chance to prove myself to Jacob. But Michael didn't need to know that. Jessica and Ashley realized I had a thing for Jacob but were staying clear and not interfering. Now with Michael's presence, everything was more complicated.

But that didn't make it impossible.

Michael strolled along both sides of the aisle way, checking the status of the stalls. He stopped at

Killer's. The little devil on my shoulder hoped the horse would bite him. Michael stretched out his arm, and Killer walked to him, making a sound that seemed like a greeting. His massive head came over the gate as he nuzzled Michael's face. The big cowboy stroked the animal's neck and scratched his forehead.

Jacob walked over to join his brother and put a hand on his shoulder. "Killer has sure missed you. I think he became more cantankerous every day you were gone."

From a pocket, Michael produced a peppermint which disappeared in an instant on a long tongue. "Unlike the rest of my family, who were probably happier before I got here."

Jacob chuckled. "Nah. We're always glad to see you, bro. Appreciate you coming. You know that."

A touching scene, and one in which I didn't belong. Invisibility seemed to be my super power but not in a good way.

I spent the rest of the day doing outside chores, due to the stench that clung to me. I raked the last of the dead leaves from the flower beds around the chuck wagon and bunk house, greeting guests from a respectful distance as they came and went from the day's trail ride.

During the ride, I cleaned out Killer's stall. He seldom went out when guests were around, because no one could handle him. But Michael led today's ride, and Jacob had the back end of the group. The mysterious brother certainly rode tall in the saddle, and the big chestnut stallion appeared proud to be in the spotlight. Michael seemed to do everything with assurance, and more than that, with an attitude of daring anyone to question him.

I noticed the visitors weren't laughing and cutting up as much today as they were earlier in the week. Michael might look good—not that I cared—but I was afraid his arrogant attitude would ruin everything his siblings had built up.

Ashley and Jessica took care of me, bringing me water and a sack lunch which I ate under a massive locust tree behind the buildings. It was cold for that, but the fresh air made up for the chill. The girls sat with me for a few minutes but excused themselves sooner than they would have normally. I couldn't blame them. I assumed I smelled to the high hills and my nose had just gotten used to it.

When the trail ride was over, the horses were turned into the corral, and the guests slowly walked to the chuck wagon for dinner. I waited until they were safely inside before meeting Jacob at the fence. "Hey. How did the ride go?"

He seemed lost in thought, but my question jerked him back. "Oh, good. Great. Michael took the lead today."

"Yes, I saw that when you headed out."

"Oh. I mean, he took the lead on everything. Where we went, when we rested, where we broke for lunch, what stories were told. Just took the lead. Not that I mind. I'm glad to have him here. It was just different."

"You can't let him walk all over you, Jacob. If you don't like the way he's doing things here, you should speak up. All three of you should. There's only one of him. Surely, he'd listen to you since you've been running the business successfully all these months. I don't know how he can expect to just show up and take over. You shouldn't let him."

Jacob smiled weakly. "You don't understand, Hannah. There's more to it than you know."

I took a deep breath to calm myself. "Tell me, so I can understand. I do have a vested interest, after all." *I'm in love with the kind brother.*

Michael walked around the corner of the barn, frowning. "Vested interest, eh? I didn't know we had sold shares in the Rocking H."

It was more than a little bit awkward that he had heard me encouraging Jacob to stand up to him, but I wasn't afraid of Michael. I took a step closer to him, staring up into his face. I hoped I smelled horrible.

"Ha ha. I work here, and I care what happens to the ranch. I care what happens to the people who own it too. At least, three of them."

A moment passed in which Jacob looked afraid of what would happen, and then Michael threw back his head and laughed. Some of the horses raised their heads from their grazing and stared at him.

"You're frightening the stock," I said.

He finally got himself under control, and Jacob's face had relaxed into bemusement. "Ms. Kincaid, you're as transparent as a mountain stream. I know exactly what's going on in that pretty little red head of yours. Now, it's close enough to quitting time. Why don't you climb into your car and go on home?"

I looked from him to Jacob. Was I being fired?

But Jacob didn't look all that concerned. "Yeah, Hannah. You've worked hard today. We'll see you tomorrow. Last day for this bunch of guests, and we want to end the week with the usual hoopla."

My heart rate started to slow back to normal. I wasn't losing my job.

Michael had accidentally opened up possibilities to me when he pushed me into the more active role I wanted. Hopefully, manure wouldn't be a daily part of that role. I knew after I left, Jacob would stand up for me and straighten out his brother, once the two of them could talk quietly. I was part of the four-person team that always created a memorable last day for each group of guests. I'd be sure to arrive not only on time, but early on Saturday, to start on the best breakfast of the week.

"Okay. Thanks, Jacob. See you in the morning." I ignored Michael completely, especially since he looked like he was going to speak. I sashayed to my car, hoping one or both of them noticed. Jacob because I wanted him to think of me as his girlfriend, and Michael because—

Well, I wasn't sure why.

Chapter Four

WHEN I GOT home, Mom smelled me before she saw me. She met me in the back hall, making a shooing motion with both hands. "Oh, my land! Hannah, please go back out into the garage. I'll get you something to put on. Put those stinky clothes in the washing machine and start it. And your boots…"

"I left them in the garage. There's nothing stuck to them. I got it all cleaned off at the ranch. Sorry about the smell, Mom. I got a promotion today."

She attempted a smile. "Is that what you call it? Okay, I'll be right back. I think you should take your shower here in the downstairs bathroom."

"Got it. You don't want *eau de horse* wafting through the whole house. Neither do I, believe me."

Mostly we only used the downstairs bathroom as a powder room for guests these days. Maybe now it would become my routine to clean up down here after a day at the ranch. But that wasn't a big deal. Just a part of making everything come together, so Jacob and I could do the same.

"I suppose it was only a matter of time…" Mom shook her head, her voice trailing off as she went upstairs.

I stripped, dumped all my clothes and some laundry soap in the washer, and dashed down the hall to the tiny bathroom. When I had scrubbed myself and smelled like soap, I put on jeans and a turtleneck sweater, which is what Mom had brought down for me. Any other night, I might have climbed the stairs immediately to change into sweats and a T-shirt, but today the extra trip upstairs was just too much effort. Two additional factors kept me from it—the aroma of dinner and the need to discuss the day with someone who understood. I was almost sure my parents wouldn't fulfill that need, but heck, why not try?

I returned to the kitchen where Mom was flying

through the process of creating a giant tossed salad. "We're having a mini family reunion this evening. I invited your grandmother, Jacqueline, and Nick. Emily and Isabel, too."

"Oh yeah? Awesome." Reinforcements, that's what I needed. I wasn't sure who would be most interested and supportive of my Jacob-plan, but I'd find out. A phone call to Taylor was also a possibility, as long as it wasn't too late by the time everyone left.

Gran, Aunt Jacquie—Mom's sister—and Aunt Jacquie's husband Nick arrived together, having carpooled from town since they live next door to each other. My older sister Emily and her daughter Isabel rushed in a few minutes later. Emily apologized that they'd had a diaper emergency right when they were ready to leave their house on the tree farm. None of us minded that they were a little bit late. With a toddler, you should always be granted some leniency on being punctual, I think.

It was nice to have eight of us around the dining table, instead of just my parents and me. A surprise appearance by Taylor and Ken would have made it even better. Our brother Ben had his perfect life on the West Coast, and we hadn't seen him since Taylor's wedding. That day was still vivid in my mind—when she and Ken realized the two of them shared a bond from decades before they were born.

I gave myself a mental shake. Since when was I so all about family? What had happened to the Hannah Kincaid that couldn't wait to get out of Serendipity forever? Now I was hanging around trying to trap a cowboy—one who was awfully good at sidestepping my advances and not recognizing my charm. So far, at least. That needed to change. If it didn't, I'd go back to Plan A—get a life. Elsewhere.

I couldn't find a good point during dinner to interject my diversion of conversation. We sat over dessert for quite a while, as everyone caught up on town news, until I was ready to scream. *This*. This was a big reason not to stay in our dead-end town where we had little to do besides talk about each other.

Emily was looking at me as if expecting an answer to a question. Maybe I had tuned out a little too much. "Hello?" she said. "I asked how you're liking the dude ranch, Hannah. Francie still feels bad that she had to let you go."

Gran barely stifled a laugh, and Aunt Jacquie's eyes were sparkling. What did they know, and how did they know it? "Hannah is *very* happy at the dude ranch, aren't you, dear?" Gran said.

I scanned the others' faces. Dad, Nick, and Isabel were the only ones who didn't have a cat who ate the canary look. So maybe my attempted relationship with Jacob wasn't such a secret. I swallowed a tiny bite of cheesecake and cleared my throat. "Yes, I'm happy there. For now, anyway. I mean, it's a job and sort of in my field."

Aunt Jacquie giggled and pushed her empty dessert plate away. "Honey, it's about as much in your field as Taylor working at the antiques shop is using her marketing degree. But, oh well, right?" She took Nick's hand on the table, raised it to her lips, and kissed it. "What we do for love doesn't have to make sense."

Now Dad was interested. "What? What do you mean *love*? Hannah's job at the Rocking H is just that—a job." He eyed me. "Or am I wrong?"

Mom put her hand on his shoulder. "Very wrong, darling, but, so far, it's the unrequited sort. Isn't that right, Hannah dear?"

Good grief. I'd wanted someone to discuss my situation with, but this was more like a grilling session. "I—well—"

Nick looked from Aunt Jacquie, to Dad and Mom, to me. "Hannah fell for one of the Hollingsworth brothers?"

"Jacob," his wife answered. "She barely knows the older one, Michael."

"Oh," Nick said. "I've met both of them, just casually, of course. Not in the line of duty—seat belt infraction or anything." Nick was the city police chief. "They seem like all right guys. Both of them."

How had he met Michael when the guy had only been here for a day? "Well, you're wrong about one thing," I said. "Michael is a stuck-up, power-hungry jerk."

Aunt Jacquie sat up a little straighter, an unreadable look on her face. "Is that right?"

I should have shut up, but couldn't stop my

mouth. "Yes, it's right. He comes in for some quick trip and starts telling everybody how to do things. He went on a trail ride with Jacob but insisted on leading it and made Jacob take the tail. The four of us were better off before he arrived. Everything was running smoothly."

Gran was next to me, and took my hand in hers. "They're siblings so, of course, there will be some disagreements. That's perfectly normal."

Emily, wiping dinner off Isabel's face, piped up. "You can't expect to run the show, Hannah. I'm sure you're doing a good job for them but, remember, you're the employee and the four of them are the partners who own the business. I'm afraid you're going to get yourself riled up, so angry at Michael, and say something you might regret."

Dad nodded. "Yes. Something that will lose your job for you before you've found something more professional per your long-range plan."

Mom slid a pitying look his way. Dad was holding on to my original hopes and dreams, and I was grateful to him for that. Mom, however, seemed aware of my current strategy—make Jacob wake up and see the real me.

But how? Oh yeah, that's what I was going to discuss with…somebody receptive. Everyone at the table had an opinion about the dude ranch, its owners, and my place in it. Whether any of them could see my side, I wasn't sure.

"So, guys, here's my situation. I'm at the Rocking H six days a week, do my job, interact with everybody in a positive manner. I keep hoping Jacob will wake up one day and realize I'm the woman for him. I mean, how hard can it be? I'm the only one there who isn't transient or related to him."

"Plus cute as a button," Gran said.

"Thanks, Gran. Really, I'm at a loss, and open to suggestions."

Dad coughed. "I'm pretty sure you don't want or expect my input. There's a game on, so I'll excuse myself." He looked at his brother-in-law. "Nick?"

Nick's look of relief was almost comical. He quickly slid out his chair and, in a moment, the two of them had gone to the living room and turned on the TV.

Isabel started squirming to get down and banged

her spoon on the highchair tray. Mom spoke soothingly to her and took her out of the chair, balancing the toddler on her lap and entertaining her with the small toys kept nearby for that purpose. "Sweetheart," she said. "I think you just need to be completely honest with Jacob. Tell him what your feelings are and find out whether he reciprocates. Otherwise, you may be biding your time there for no reason at all."

What a ridiculous idea. Was Mom that out of touch with reality? "Gee Mom. Really? Just ask him? Is that how you got Dad to notice you?"

"That was entirely different, and it went the other way round. He had to pester me forever to get my attention." She sighed, smiling in reminiscence.

"Okay, but back to the real world," Aunt Jacquie said. "Do you want me to talk to him, Hannah? Not browbeat him, but just, you know, get a vibe about where his head is?"

Why did she suddenly sound like an escapee from the 1960s? But I knew Aunt Jacquie did get vibes or whatever from people, and she had about a perfect score of knowing what was going on with them. "I'll see if I can get him into your shop, Aunt Jacquie. Moving Jacob off the ranch during the day is unlikely, but I'll give it my best. Or…you could drop by?"

She tipped her head to one side, considering. "Go out to the ranch and visit? Hmm. Sure, I think that can be arranged," she said. "Let me know what times he'll be around so I can get him alone for a few minutes' conversation."

Here at last was potential movement toward my goal. "Absolutely. The guests leave tomorrow before noon, so he'll have some free time in the afternoon. Awesome, Aunt Jacquie!"

Emily was shaking her head. "What?" I asked, exasperated.

"Oh, I don't know. I almost lean toward Mom's honesty is the best policy idea. I'm not saying you should blurt out *My heart is yours. Are you even interested?* But something more diplomatic that could get you the same answer."

"Hey, at this point, I'm not sure I can manage diplomacy. I have Michael pushing my buttons at every opportunity, Ashley and Jessica keeping their heads down and trying not to irritate him, and Jacob blithely unaware of..." My voice trailed off. I'd been about to say Jacob was unaware of me. I thought back to his question about whether I had cleaned out stalls before. "Anyway, I'll go with Aunt Jacquie's offer."

Emily nodded. "I hear you. She's got a pretty high percentage rating except for the one person she couldn't figure out."

We all laughed at that, remembering the surprise when Jacqueline and Nick had ended up together after years of separation and distrust.

Gran sipped from her water glass and when she set it down, the ice clinked. Her silence meant something.

"Okay, Gran. Tell me what you think. You're the wisest person here, I'm sure we all agree."

She smiled. "Hannah dear, I believe you know what I think. But I'll say it out loud if you insist. If Jacob is the man for you, the two of you will discover that naturally. Pushing too hard sometimes results in pushing someone away. It's been decades since your grandfather and I dated, but I find it hard to believe that basic facts have changed drastically." She sighed, folded her cloth napkin, and placed it on the table. "Still, you will do what you think is best. That's one of the wonderful things about being a grandmother. I'm here to provide support and encouragement, but you don't really have to ask for my opinion. And having heard it, you don't need to abide by it." She grinned. "At my age, there's peace in knowing that what will be, will be."

Isabel yawned enormously and I couldn't help doing the same. Emily rose and stretched. "Must get my girl to bed. David will be home for the weekend in a couple of hours, and I want her to be sound asleep so he and I get some private time." Her cheeks turned pink, and I brushed off the instant desire to be in her position.

I didn't want to have Emily's life. It was perfect for her and, in spite of our history a few years ago, I was glad she and David were so happy together. I didn't envy what or whom she had but wanted the life that was right for me. Gran's pronouncement of *what will be, will be* didn't come across as encouraging at all. Hopefully, Aunt Jacquie's intervention would provide a turning point for Jacob and me.

Chapter Five

THE ROCKING H Saturday breakfast was a huge deal each week. It was the last opportunity to make a great impression on the dude ranch guests. The idea was to send them off with stomachs pleasantly full of delicious down-home food, a smile on their faces, and the urge to spread the word about the ranch to everyone they knew.

Word of mouth advertising is powerful. Everyone in a small town knows that. Whether it's good news, like an awesome week at a dude ranch, or bad news, like a piece of ugly gossip, one-on-one sharing of information is without compare in its effectiveness.

I set my alarm half an hour earlier than usual and set my phone alarm too, so I'd be sure to get up and moving. I didn't want to endure another scene like yesterday's.

Shaking my head to try to jar myself awake after a night filled with dreams of tall cowboys, I crawled out of bed. My muscles were screaming from the physical exertion of cleaning out the stalls. Getting dressed was agony but, finally, I pulled on jeans, a long-sleeve shirt, and warm socks.

I descended the stairs slowly and poured a mug of coffee in the kitchen. Mom was preparing dinner— her usual workday routine, filling the slow cooker before heading to the consignment store on the square. When the coffee kicked in and I could speak coherently, we talked about the play they had tickets for in New Albany tonight. They had invited me along but, as usual, I'd be staying home. I filled my mug again for the road, ready to leave. At the back door by the coat hooks, I stopped and groaned. My brown work jacket wasn't there.

"Mom, you didn't happen to wash my Carhartt, did you?"

"No, honey. Where is it?"

Just what I'd feared. "Ugh. On the floor next to the washer. I forgot about it 'til just now. I'll have to wear this pink puffy thing." I jerked a thumb toward the nylon fashion statement I'd bought for college. "I'll look ridiculous."

She put the lid on the slow cooker and faced me. "I wondered what the smell was in the garage but thought maybe your boots weren't as clean as you thought. Well, throw the work jacket into the washer and start it on your way out, honey. I'll dry it before I go to the store."

I thanked her and did as she asked and pulled on the pink jacket which said ski bunny more than horse wrangler. I started the car and headed for the ranch, occasionally sipping coffee while I cursed Michael under my breath. Despite my good intentions, I was only going to be about fifteen minutes early. I wasn't late often, and when I was, I stayed over in the evening or took less time for lunch. No one had made an issue about it until now. Michael was a real pain in the rear.

I had hoped his showing up would give Jacob more time for me, but if yesterday was an indication, that might not be the case. I'd hardly seen Jacob at all, and when I did, Michael interrupted our brief conversation—one during which I smelled like manure. Not exactly ideal, even though it sort of went along with my wish to become more a part of the overall operation. By the time my coffee mug was drained and I pulled onto Rocking H property, I'd convinced myself that today would be the turning point for Jacob and me.

Breakfast preparations had begun, but I stepped in and did my part as usual. The three of us were a great team. Jacob didn't help in the kitchen except occasionally if we were in a time crunch. I'd seen him near the corral when I parked my car. He seemed to be talking, so I assumed Michael was standing near him but out of my sight. If only he was *always* out of my sight.

Jessica and Ashley had been exchanging glances. Once we had everything ready for the guests to appear, Jessica looked around to be sure we were still the only ones in the kitchen-great room area. She looked to Ashley and put a gentle hand on my arm. "We're so glad you're here today, Hannah. After what

Michael put you through yesterday, we wondered."

"I hope you know I wouldn't get my feelings hurt and just fail to show up. And on a Saturday? Come on."

"Yes, but Michael…"

I shrugged. "He's an irritant, like a mosquito. You think you're ready. You've sprayed yourself so they won't bother you, and then *zing*, they bite. I'm familiar with how it works. From now on, I won't let Michael bother me."

The girls' eyes had grown large as I spoke the last few words, and I knew what was coming next.

"It's good to hear I'm not bothering you, Hannah," Michael said.

I took a steadying breath and turned to face him. Jacob was next to him, looking embarrassed. As was typical, they had toed off their boots at the entry, and were walking sock-footed, not making any noise.

I knew I wasn't the only one who wished Michael would chill out. The three normal siblings had to feel the same way. "Great," I said brightly. "You do your work, and I'll do mine."

"As long as you're actually *doing* your work." He raised one dark brow, looking like a villain in a horror movie.

Jacob nudged him. "Hey, Michael, go a little easy on her, okay? Hannah is one of us."

That made me feel like singing. *One of us*—yay.

Michael looked long and hard at Jacob and gave him a wry smile. "If you say so. We're still a go with the cross-training, right? Hannah learned to clean out the stalls yesterday. Today—"

"Michael, not today," Jessica said. "Give her some time to recuperate."

Great idea, as I knew my speed in the kitchen was affected by my sore muscles. I needed to be sure not to groan out loud while serving the guests.

Saturday was pretty predictable. After lots of photos and fond farewells, the four of us would thoroughly clean the bunk house and chuck wagon. Depending on the weather and circumstances, there might be yard work and small repair projects too. Would Michael participate in all that and be constantly underfoot and irritating everyone? I had Sundays off, but knew the stables got attention on Sunday afternoons. I was ashamed to wish that continued. I didn't relish the thought of reconnecting with the pitchfork any time soon.

What was I thinking? I wanted to be involved in every facet of the operation. Bring on the pitchfork, if that was what it took.

The guests straggled into the room dressed in their returning-to-normal-life clothes instead of the jeans and Western shirts they'd worn during the last five days. They all looked a little sad, which was typical. They spoke softly, reminiscing about adventures they'd experienced together during the week. We cheered them up with feather-light pancakes, two kinds of sausage, bacon, and biscuits and gravy. For those who wanted healthier fare, we served oatmeal, granola, yogurt, and fruit. We also provided grapefruit juice, orange juice, and as Jacob said at least once a day, the best coffee in the county.

For this meal only, we sat with the guests, answering questions, laughing as they took selfies with a stack of pancakes, nodding as they swore they would come back again next year.

Watching Michael during this meal was like seeing a different person entirely. He laughed easily, listened well, and seemed genuinely interested in everyone he spoke to. The guests were drawn to him, maybe even more than they were to Jacob. He had a charisma, much as I dislike that word, that was undeniable.

We walked outside with the guests, helping where needed with suitcases and bags of purchases made in Serendipity on their occasional ventures to town shops. I saw a couple of paper sacks with the Once Upon a Time logo on them and even one from Emily's Dreams, the consignment shop were Mom worked. As expected by those who ponder such things, the dude ranch was good business for more than just the Rocking H.

The last SUV finally pulled out of the driveway and the five of us expelled a collective sigh of relief.

"This is the best job in the world," Jessica said. "But being here without the tenderfeet is a treat. It's relaxing, even though we have a day and a half of almost constant work before the next group shows up."

Ashley nodded. "I feel like going for a ride before we start cleaning. Anybody with me?"

"I'm in," said Jacob, starting for the barn with her.

Jessica looked to me and I waved her on, glad for them to have a good time after all their hard work. "Yep, me too," she said, smiling and sending me a little wink.

This left me standing next to Michael. "You go ahead," I said. "This happens a lot of Saturdays."

"They go riding and you do what?"

I wouldn't let his tone bother me. Instead, I turned away from him and tossed my answer over my shoulder. "Lay by the fire and eat bon-bons. Nap for a couple of hours. What else?"

Once inside, I toed off my boots and set them by the wall, slipped off my silly pink jacket, and hung it on a hook. After retrieving my long apron from the kitchen, I got the cart and started cleaning up the breakfast mess. Instead of being angry at Michael's question, I shrugged it off. Like a mosquito. It was as easy as I had said, and I was glad for the analogy.

When I had gathered all the dirty dishes, silverware, and napkins and was rolling the cart back to the kitchen, I half expected Michael to be there standing in my way, prepared to say something to tick me off. It seemed he was always doing that.

But I was still the only one in the building. I told myself that suited me fine. I was glad to be spared another episode with him. Still, the place seemed lonely, and that wasn't a feeling that had occurred to me before. I wondered what he was doing if he hadn't decided to go for a ride after all.

Something bright caught my eye when I glanced out the window, and I recognized Aunt Jacquie's shining red hair. She was bundled in a navy pea coat, standing in the parking lot, and having what looked like a pleasant conversation with Michael.

I was frustrated that she was here when Jacob was not, and if history was a predictor, he and his sisters would be gone for at least a couple of hours.

Aunt Jacquie has a sixth sense about people. But I had wasted her time today with no one but the dreaded

Michael to put under her microscope.

Chapter Six

A WHILE LATER, Aunt Jacquie came into the kitchen. "Hey there. Could I give you a hand with this?"

"No, that's okay. It only looks like a national disaster area. I've got it under control. This is kind of my usual Saturday, and I don't mind. It's almost peaceful. How about you sit on one of the stools and talk to me while I work?"

She drew up a tall stool from its location on the far side of the bar window. "I had a nice chat with Michael. Sorry I missed Jacob." She didn't say that she would try to catch him another time, but I assumed she would make good on her promise to talk to him.

"Yeah. Silly on my part. Ninety percent of the time, he's gone by this time on Saturday."

"Michael is worried about you, Hannah."

A dish almost slipped out of my hand. I caught it, steadied my breath, and met her gaze. "I'm sorry. It sounded like you said *Michael* is worried about *me*."

She nodded, her hair swinging. "That's it. Not what he said out loud, but you know I can read between the lines."

"Yeah. Like nobody else in the world."

"That might be going a little far, but I'll let it slide." She shot a look behind her out the window where the parking area opened to the barnyard. "He went into the barn, to see what needs to be done. So he won't overhear us. Anyway, Michael worries that you're looking for something here that you won't find and, eventually, you'll move on because of disappointment."

"Is he going to stand between Jacob and me?"

"Honey. There *is* no relationship between Jacob and you. There is only your wish for one. Michael knows that."

"Huh? How the heck does he know that?"

"Because your emotions are plainly displayed on your face, Hannah. The world at large knows you want Jacob. He's the only one who doesn't realize it, and there's a good reason for that."

"Which is?"

Michael was striding briskly across the parking area, toward the building where we were. Aunt Jacquie saw him too. "I'm sorry I wasn't able to do what you wanted, Hannah. I do have a strong feeling that everything is going to turn out very well for you. Not the way you expect, so you need to be flexible and ready to embrace new possibilities."

Aargh. The sixties again. "Okay. Thanks for coming out, Aunt Jacquie. Do you want a cup of coffee or anything? Jacob says it's the best in the county."

She laughed and stood. "No thanks. I'll go make some in my French press that puts Jacob's brew to shame. Don't worry so much about what Jacob thinks and says, honey." She gave me a quick hug around my sudsy hands and excused herself. In a moment I heard her and Michael talking. I guess they met by the front door.

Then he was in the kitchen, his presence making it seem smaller.

"Your aunt is nice. She seemed worried about you."

"Have mercy. Is everybody worried about me? I'm completely fine! I think you all need to just think about something else."

He put up his hands as if in defense of me possibly spraying him with dish water. When he decided that wasn't going to happen, he sank onto the stool Aunt Jacquie had just vacated. "I'm glad the rest of them went on a ride. It gives me a chance to talk to you alone."

Was he going to try to fire me and send me on my way when there was no one to explain, again, that I was a valued employee? Well, I wouldn't be dismissed that easily. I'd stand up to him.

On his feet again, he paced the short distance between cabinets while I tried to concentrate on cleaning leftover gunk off the sausage pan.

"Here's the thing, Hannah. Jacob is in a

relationship with someone else."

My stomach clutched and the pan sank to the bottom of the sink. "He's—what? And, well, if he is…in a relationship…why tell *me* that?"

He rolled his eyes. "Let's skip the part where you pretend you're not interested in my brother, okay?"

I counted to ten to be sure I could control my tone of voice. "I'm not going to say anything about it."

"He's known this girl—Christy—for years. I'm talking since childhood. Her family owned the ranch next to us in Montana. Jacob and Christy were an item most of their lives. She became an incredibly talented horsewoman. Won all the local and regional championships growing up. Once she graduated high school, she started traveling the country, competing for the big purses in barrel racing and what have you. From what I've heard, she did well. She and Jacob didn't actually break up; they just went separate ways. The rest of us wrote her off but, evidently, he always hoped she would come back to him. In time, Mom and Dad sold our ranch and retired. Her parents did the same. The four of them have set up a kind of Montana outpost in the Florida suburbs. It's—unique." He smiled briefly at the image.

Heart pounding, my fantasy romance with Jacob slipped away with each word Michael spoke. I didn't want to believe him, but it was too wild a story for him to make up and think he could get away with it. "And now she's ready to come back to Jacob?"

He watched me carefully, judging my reaction. "Maybe. She got hurt pretty badly at a show. She's been in the hospital for several weeks, and Jacob got in touch and told her there's a place for her here. She doesn't want to go to her parents because they begged her not to live that life. Competing as a kid was one thing, but they want her to be done with it. Grow out of it."

I believed in pursuing your passion. It seemed the only way to live an honest life was to do what you felt strongly about and particularly suited to. Aunt Jacquie was an example of someone who had always done just that. When she came back to Serendipity and fell in love with Nick, her passion didn't die. She just found a different outlet for it.

In a moment, I found my voice. "If Christy is following her dream, it's not really something you grow out of."

Michael nodded. "Exactly, and that's what it was for Christy."

"Is she going to be okay?" I couldn't help caring about this young woman who had chased her dreams against all odds.

"Should be, but no more competitions. At least, that's the way I understand it from Jacob. As you can imagine, he was pretty torn up when he called and asked me to come."

"He asked you to come to Serendipity?"

"Yes. To learn how they've been running the ranch, so when Christy arrives, if Jacob needs to drive her to rehab during the week, or whatever, I can fill in for him."

"Oh." It was all I could say. My hope had been for Jacob to have more time for me, when all the while he was pining for the woman he loved. I breathed deeply, expecting a stabbing pain at the loss of Jacob. But where I thought my love for Jacob had resided, there was just a dull, empty ache. Had it really been love or just a crush because he was so kind and handsome?

Michael stopped pacing, his face quizzical. "You're taking it pretty well. Better than I expected, I must say."

I was relieved Michael couldn't read my mind. One minute I thought I was in love with his brother, and the next one I realized what a fool I had made of myself trying to get Jacob to fall for me. "Well, I'm not completely heartless. If Jacob and this girl love each other, I'm happy for them." I sagged against the counter as another thought hit me. "I guess in a perverse way this is a relief, because, otherwise, I must have absolutely no ability to attract a man."

He shook his head, laughing. "No worries there, Hannah. None at all."

In another situation, with another man, I would take his statement as a compliment. "Is her arrival going to mean I'll be in the way?"

He picked up a dish towel and started to dry. "Quite the opposite. Your ability to pitch in where needed will help us keep the ranch running smoothly. We all care about Christy and must respect Jacob's wish to do everything he can for her. But we also have to make sure our guests still get the enjoyable experience they pay for."

I looked up at him. "Which is why you've been pushing the cross-training when you knew it was just aimed at me."

"Yep."

A chunk of dislike fell off the wall I had built between Michael and myself. "Why not just say so?"

He shrugged. "Because I didn't know you. And Jacob hadn't told the girls about Christy. He's breaking that news right about now, or at least he promised he would. They used to be close friends, and I know the girls still love her. But Jess and Ashley haven't forgiven her for dumping our besotted brother back in the day." He hung the pan on its hook and faced me. "Once they know what happened to Christy, and that Jacob wants her here, I think it'll all work out."

His sisters' ignorance of the situation was good news. I considered Jessica and Ashley my friends, and if they'd withheld the information about Christy's arrival, that would have hurt.

He continued, "Even with Jess and Ashley in the dark on why I showed up, they seemed happy enough about me being here. But, in a way, they were probably afraid I'd try to run the place. It's typical behavior since I'm the oldest, but we're adults now."

This conversation that had started so strangely now felt intimate, helped by the shared task with the dishes. "How could you just pick up from wherever and come play cowboy?"

He sighed, shot a look to the ceiling. "If I tell you, do you promise not to hate me?"

What a reaction. Had I been right when I suggested to Taylor that he had a shady past? "I think so."

Michael hung up his dish towel and crossed his arms. "I retired a couple of years ago, and I've been traveling."

"Ha. Retired?"

He shrugged. "I'm pretty smart with money, plus I invented something that I sold to one of the big electronics companies."

"You retired at the age of—"

He nodded. "Twenty-seven. Some people instantly hate me when I say that. Thank goodness, it doesn't come up often. I travel, so I meet new folks all the time. Everybody's on vacation, and I can sidestep questions about what I do by saying what I *used* to do. Invent stuff. Work on a dude ranch."

He retired at twenty-seven, and at twenty-three, I hadn't started my career yet. "That makes me feel like a complete loser."

The corners of his eyes crinkled when he smiled, something I hadn't noticed since he didn't smile much around me. "It shouldn't make you feel like a loser. It's just what worked out for me, you know? For Jacob and my sisters, this kind of place is what they always wanted. Too bad we didn't all realize how much they would miss ranch life when our parents planned to sell. Although a ranch this size, in a climate that doesn't get feet of snow every year, is a lot easier for them to handle. And, Serendipity seems an all right town to live near. No mountains, though. I miss the mountains."

Even though I'd never lived near them, hearing him say that and seeing the faraway look in his eyes, made me miss the mountains too.

It was one of the strangest conversations I'd ever been part of, one in which my objective of attracting Jacob went flying out the window at the same time my wish to be more a part of the ranch's operation was granted.

I thought I understood family dynamics, having grown up in one that had occasional, and some long-term, dysfunction. But Michael had dropped everything in order to help his siblings keep their business afloat while also enabling them to provide recuperation for the woman who'd turned her back on the whole family. What kind of man did that? What kind of really rich, early retiree wouldn't just hire an experienced cowboy or two and continue with the travel he obviously enjoyed? The more I got to know him, the more Michael Hollingsworth seemed an enigma.

When his siblings returned, it was obvious the Christy Conversation had taken place. Jacob looked happy—after all he was getting his girlfriend back.

Jessica and Ashley didn't say much, but looked at me with pity in their eyes. It wasn't necessary though. My Jacob plan was gone, but since the talk with Michael I had recovered enough to remember I didn't want to hang around Serendipity anyway.

I threw myself into cleaning every inch of the chuck wagon and guest rooms. When quitting time finally arrived, I pulled on the puffy pink jacket that screamed I didn't belong on a dude ranch. With my hand on the doorknob, I managed a cheerful tone when saying I would see them Monday morning. They all replied in kind, as if nothing unusual had transpired today.

Except Michael, who watched me with a different sort of look in his eyes.

Chapter Seven

THE NEXT FEW weeks passed in a blur. Thanksgiving came and went, ringing in the overeating season along with holiday festivity. We decorated the Rocking H in red ribbon and tinsel from the front gate posts to the great room mantle. As the weeks marched toward Christmas, each group of guests became more upbeat and happy to be outside no matter the temperature. They were also happy to sit around the fire and tell outrageous lies about their horseback riding exploits.

I blamed it partly on the eggnog of which Jessica refused to divulge all the ingredients.

The only person who wasn't in the Christmas spirit was Jacob, and he had a decent reason. He was yearning for Christy. She had finally been released from the hospital, but her parents had insisted on her spending the season in their home.

One day after talking to her on the phone in the chuck wagon, he burst out, "She hates Florida. She's always hated Florida. I can't think why her parents are making her stay with them."

Jessica put an arm around his shoulders. "Because they care about her too, Jacob. Come on, they probably even feel guilty for giving her such a rough time when she left. Things between them were pretty ugly there for a while, remember? Let them mend their fences, make up with her. You know she's looking forward to coming up here."

"Yeah, I know. It's just that I wanted to take care of her."

"Honey, you aren't going to tame a girl like Christy by tying her shoes for her," Jessica said. "You know that, right?"

He looked up, his face coloring. "I'm not trying to tame her." Then his shoulders sagged. "Okay, maybe that is what I had in mind."

Ashley joined them. "It'll work out, Jacob. I

know this is the right time for you and Christy. You've both had some growing up to do, don't you think? And the rest of us needed time to forgive her."

A grin pulled at one corner of his lip. "Yeah, probably. Hey, Hannah, did I tell you that when I go to Mom and Dad's for Christmas, I'll bring Christy back with me?"

"That's awesome, Jacob. I'm really looking forward to meeting her."

But Jacob hadn't shared that news with me until just now. Michael had told me yesterday afternoon as we cleaned out stalls together. It had become our peaceful, if smelly, catch-up time, and I weirdly looked forward to it. I had found an old coat at the consignment shop and kept it in my car for those days. I didn't want to have to wash my Carhartt every time I pulled stable duty.

****

Michael was in the habit of taking the horses out to the corral without asking if I wanted to do it. He never pushed me to deal with the horses, nor made fun of me for being especially afraid of Killer. He closed the corral gate behind the last one and walked toward me where I waited in the barn for him. Tall, handsome, still tanned from the last sunny place he'd traveled to.

And, though I'd disliked him at first, I knew now that Michael was a very nice guy.

The more time I spent with him, the more I realized I had misjudged him. I blamed him early on for keeping me and Jacob apart and for expecting more of me on the ranch than I was capable of. But as I found peace with the reality of Jacob's love life, I also realized Michael hadn't pushed me any harder than he would have any other employee.

From what I could see, he worked harder and longer than any of the rest of us. Maybe his early retirement wasn't just a lucky shot. Perhaps he'd failed to mention that he'd put forth a huge effort and was rewarded for it. I needed to work harder at trying to find the first step in my career. Time was wasting, and my presence on the ranch wasn't critical. Someone else could walk in and do as well or better without a lot of training. I'd been mistaken to hang around here waiting for Jacob and, even though I was fond of everyone at the Rocking H, that wasn't a reason to hang on forever.

Smiling, Michael tapped me on the shoulder to get my attention. "I appreciate your willingness to pitch in and help with this least pleasant task, Hannah."

I shrugged. "Well, it's certainly one of those jobs where you know you've accomplished something. Everyone within twenty feet knows I've accomplished it too."

He laughed. "For somebody who doesn't like horses, you're a fine ranch hand."

"I like horses. I'm just not one hundred percent sure how they feel about me." Mostly I was thinking of Killer when I said that. He always watched me so carefully, as if planning my demise.

"What is it you really want to do, Hannah? I'm embarrassed I haven't asked before now." He looked at me as if he cared about my answer.

It was as if he'd read my thoughts. "Well, my degree is environmental management. Nothing has come along for me there yet, so for now, I'm grateful to have this job and good friends." A few weeks ago I wouldn't have included Michael among my friends, but he was now. I enjoyed spending time with him. Looked forward to it.

His brows rose in surprise. "Environmental management? That's great. So many things you can do with it. I know some people…" He stopped, looking thoughtful. "So, how far are you willing to move for the right position?"

With the holidays and the impending arrival of Christy, I hadn't paid much attention lately to the online postings. When I thought about it, I wasn't sure the last time I had checked. "Oh, anywhere in the country, I guess. My Aunt Jacquie used to be a travel writer. I always thought it must be awesome to go all over the country, seeing new things. I know I wouldn't be doing that, but I'd like to visit new places."

"But Serendipity will always be home, right?"

When I'd graduated in the spring, contemplating Serendipity as the center of my world was laughable. But not now. "Yes, this will always be the place I come back to, at least to visit a few times a year. My brother Ben will be in for Christmas. We haven't seen him since this summer when Taylor and Ken got married. That's just too long. I wouldn't let that much time pass before seeing my family."

Why was I spilling my guts to this guy? It seemed every time we worked together, I said more than I meant to. Did he think me ridiculously sentimental or maybe that I didn't have anyone to confide in?

"You're easier to talk to than I would have expected, Michael. If I ever babble on more than you're interested in hearing, just say so and I'll shut up."

He stopped what he was doing, and pinned me with a hot look. My skin flushed under his gaze. "I would never tell you to shut up," he said. "I want to hear your stories, learn what's important to you. And—about your career. I get the idea you're biding your time here because of what I shared about Christy. Seriously, if you find the right position and need to go, just say the word. We'll be okay. We'll find someone and make do. Don't let us slow you down, Hannah."

It was a strange offer from a self-made multimillionaire. "Okay. I'll try not to let you hold me back from reaching my full potential." I chuckled, but it sounded hollow even to me. Because in the soothing warmth of the barn, in our soft words and shared task, I realized something else was going on here. I'd fallen for Michael.

I groaned inwardly. My stupid heart was going to drive me crazy. First, a crush on Jacob who only had eyes for Christy, and now a crush on Michael who was the most inaccessible man I was likely to ever meet. He was here for a short while, and when he wasn't needed anymore, would continue to travel.

I wasn't long-term at the ranch either and had no idea where I was heading. Yeah, wishing for a future with Michael would be a big mistake.

When we finished putting fresh straw in the last stall, we high-fived each other as usual. Michael held my hand a little longer than expected, and when I looked up into his eyes, I saw not just laughter, but desire. My breath caught. Was he going to kiss me?

But he released my hand and took a step back. "Sorry, Hannah. I almost got carried away for a minute. I'd better get on with..." The end of his sentence was lost, torn away on the wind as he hurried out of the barn, leaving the door swinging.

Chapter Eight

EXCEPT FOR SOME exciting nightly dreams and a few glimpses at a distance, I didn't see Michael for the next several days. I knew he must be avoiding me on purpose. Getting romantic with the temporary help wouldn't be his style, I was sure.

That was admirable, except I had an idea I'd like for him to get romantic. What would it be like to be held in Michael's strong arms? Would his kisses make me tingle all over? Would I want him to continue even if that was a bad idea because we had no future together? Would we set aside reality, and our wildly different life paths, and give in to passion?

I kept wondering, and he kept avoiding.

But the ranch wasn't big enough for us to both

work there and not interact. One evening after dinner, he hung around the chuck wagon and started singing Christmas carols in a pleasant baritone with the guests. At one point, Jacob made an urgent signal to him and dragged the rest of us all into the kitchen as well.

"What the heck, bro?" Michael asked when all five of us were jammed in there and the door to the chuck wagon was closed.

Jacob's face was flushed. "Christmas. In Florida. We're all invited."

Jessica shook her head and reached for the eggnog. "Sure, we're invited, but we can't go. At least, not all of us can. We understand you're going down— you have to, so Christy can ride back with you. But the rest of us, or at least some of us, have to stay here and take care of the ranch."

"Don't you want to see Mom and Dad?" Jacob asked.

Jessica's eyes snapped. "Sure I do, but I have responsibilities." After being silent for a moment, her face brightened. "Listen, how about two of us go for a few days, come back, and the other two fly down? That could work, right?"

Jacob shook his head, reminding me of a spoiled child. Had he always been so stubborn and I hadn't seen it? "But we wouldn't all be together."

Michael frowned. "Jacob, you're not being realistic. Dude ranch, remember? Horses need to be fed and watered, exercised. Buildings need to be watched in case it gets a little colder. Electricity goes out and pipes freeze at the most inconvenient times, you know."

But even Michael looked a bit wistful at the thought of the four of them spending Christmas with their parents.

"I don't suppose there's any possibility of your parents coming here for the holiday?" I asked.

They all shook their heads.

Michael said, "Once they moved to Florida, they wanted nothing to do with cold weather. All their lives ranching, winter was a struggle—something to be endured, overcome."

Jessica said, "Plus, they keep hinting about a joint Christmas with Christy's folks. Like the old days."

I spoke before I could think better of it. "Well,

how about I watch things here? That way all four of you can spend a few days with your parents, without having to rush or worry."

Jacob seemed astounded. "You'd do that for us?"

Jessica was near tears. "Hannah, it's a wonderful offer, but we couldn't take advantage of you like that."

I chuckled. "You know you want to, and I've become reasonably competent. Even Michael will admit it, right?"

He nodded slowly. Was there a glimmer of the light that had been in his eyes that day in the barn? "Competent and selfless. But what about your own family holiday?"

"I'm right here, a five-minute-drive from home. I can easily keep an eye on the horses and buildings and still enjoy my Christmas." I hoped my smile looked sincere. As I watched Michael's face, I knew I was going to miss him much more than the others.

I had to admit, at least to myself, that this wasn't just a crush. I had fallen in love with the big brother. I gulped, and turned away from all of them, plugging in the kettle to make a cup of tea I didn't want. I couldn't afford for Michael or any of them to see the truth on my face. He wouldn't be in Serendipity permanently. He'd made it clear that once Christy made a full recovery and Jacob was able to do his regular work, Michael would go back to his travels.

Back to being retired and interested in everything and everyone. Back to knowing people who might hire someone with my degree. Not just anyone, but me.

I remembered back to the day we'd had that talk, when he asked what I wanted to do. I'd told him, and he said he knew some people. Why hadn't I pursued the job lead? But no, I had let that part of the day slip my mind and concentrated, instead, on the almost-kiss. Or what I, at least, imagined was an almost-kiss. Maybe I had misread him and he had hurried out of the barn for some other reason. At any rate, if I was to have another chance at learning what connections he had to people who might hire me, the conversation wouldn't happen with everyone circled around. And I'd been told that nobody hired during the Christmas season anyway. My immediate future, whether long or short, was on the Rocking H.

I had gone from hanging around the ranch, waiting for Jacob to wake up, to waiting for Prince Michael to kiss me and turn me from a frog into a career woman. I'd gotten lax at looking for online postings, thinking he might find a great job for me. And until this very moment, I hadn't realized what I was doing. Had the manure gone to my head? Michael was probably eager to leave Serendipity. The look in his eyes a few minutes ago—I'd seen it as wistful, of all things. It was probably more like wanderlust.

Like an idiot, I had fallen for the wrong guy *again*. When would I ever learn?

Chapter Nine

THE MORNING THEY were to leave, I arrived early and fixed breakfast for the five of us.

"Wow, Hannah, this is such a nice surprise," Jessica said.

"You're always cooking for and waiting on everybody else. It's your turn to relax," I said. "Your vacation has officially begun."

Michael ate quickly and excused himself to head to the barn.

"Guess he has to wish Killer a Merry Christmas," I said. The others chuckled a little, but the mood in the room was heavy and depressing. "Hey, you're going to make your parents' Christmas, you know. They're thrilled you're all coming down, right?"

Ashley nodded. "Yeah. And we'll be glad to see them. I'm so happy we get to go, and we thank you, Hannah. But it's hard to leave home. Funny, even though we've just been here a short while, it does feel like home." She looked at the beautifully decorated Standish Christmas tree in the corner of the room opposite the fireplace. "Oh! I just remembered. Presents." She scrambled out of her chair, went to the tree, and pulled a few gifts from under the back side.

My stomach sank with embarrassment. "I didn't know there were gifts under there. I thought we'd decided no gifts. I didn't buy anything," I said.

Jacob patted my hand as if I were an old lady. "You're giving us a massive gift—the free time to take this trip. But don't worry, we're paying you. Still, we couldn't go without knowing you were here to take care of everything for us." Jessica handed him a package. He nodded and handed it to me. "Here. It isn't much, but I hope you'll tolerate it because I picked it out myself."

I unwrapped the strangely shaped gift. From under dozens of layers of tissue, a small black metal horse appeared. It was wearing a red saddle and had a golden bridle and reins. "Oh, Jacob, it's darling."

"I'm glad you like it. I thought of you the minute I saw it, remembering how scared you used to be of horses, but you never stopped trying to overcome the fear."

My eyes were damp with tears. He'd realized that about me but hadn't realized I was doing it to get his attention. That was for the best and less embarrassing for me.

Jessica and Ashley each handed me a flat, identically wrapped package. Their eyes sparkled with anticipation as I opened the first one. It was a wide gold head band. "It's alpaca wool," Jessica said. "For the times you're out in the cold wind. Even if you have your hair pulled back, your ears won't get cold."

"Mine's the same," Ashley said. "Just a different color." The second one was royal blue.

The headbands were super soft and I could tell they'd feel great when I was outdoors. "Wow. Thank you both."

Michael walked in and saw what we'd been doing. He retrieved his package from under the tree and laid it in front of me on the table. "Not really what I had in mind, but I hope you can use them."

Black leather gloves, thermal lined. I slipped them on and they fit perfectly. Michael watched me, and smiled when I thanked him. But he didn't say more.

I helped Jessica and Ashley carry their suitcases to Michael's SUV. He loaded everything just so, of course. I remembered how I used to hate how precisely he did everything. Now I realized he just used his time efficiently.

I hated to see them go, but felt a real awkwardness about the goodbyes. I hugged the girls and Jacob without feeling weird, but Michael? He looked down at me after the others had climbed in. "We'll miss you, Hannah. Take care."

I waited for him to get in the car, but still he stood there. What was he waiting for? Did he want me to hug him too? I put my arms around his middle, wearing my new gloves, and gave him a quick squeeze. Instead of a return embrace, I heard an intake of breath as if my touch was poison.

I stepped back, blushing. Cripes, I wasn't that

bad, was I?

Michael turned from me and slid into the driver seat. The others shouted goodbye and waved, but Michael looked straight ahead, stepped on the gas, and left me standing there all alone.

Looked like I called that wrong. Obviously, Michael was not the touchy-feely type. From his reaction to my overture, our scene in the barn must have meant less than nothing to him.

Chapter Ten

CHRISTMAS CHANGES EVERY year now.

Back when we were kids, it seemed to always be about the same. The day after Thanksgiving, Dad would sharpen the hacksaw, and we'd pile into the van, drive to the Standish Christmas tree farm, and tromp across the hills until we found and cut the perfect tree. Back at home, we helped Mom get the decorations downstairs from the attic while Dad worked with the stand to make sure the tree would be secure and mostly vertical during the season.

The tree came down on January second. Every year. And during the holiday season, we always ate the same delicious roasted meats, starchy side dishes, vegetables with lots of cream and cheese, tiny salads, and glorious desserts. We drank hot cider and cocoa and listened to the same music every year.

Sure, the gifts changed. As we got older, there were no more dolls. We got more books and clothes and homemade gift certificates. Taylor and I especially liked each getting a certificate for a one-on-one shopping day with Mom in Louisville and a Daddy-daughter date to nearby Mendacious. Dinner at Victoria, the fancy restaurant, and a movie in the super old theater on the Mendacious square. The seats were covered in red velvet and had wooden arm rests. No cup holders—that was another tipoff that the place was old. The popcorn there was the best I've ever tasted, and I always ate a large one by myself even though I'd just had dinner.

The good old days. But so many life changes happened, and we seemed to roll with them. At Christmas, it was even more obvious how different our family life had become. The big changes started the year Emily had her wreck and had to spend the holiday at the rehab place in New Albany, about forty minutes from home. The following year she was healed but also married to David Standish, so we had to share her with the Standish family. Before her wreck, I'm sure Taylor and I never imagined we would mind sharing Emily. She wasn't particularly pleasant to be around from about the end of high school until her mid-twenties.

Soon after Emily's wedding, Ben graduated from college and moved away. None of us could forget the year everybody got snowed in when we were supposed to be going to Carla Standish's wedding at the church in town. When Isabel was born, little toys and dolls appeared once again under our tree.

This year's big difference was two-fold. Taylor was married, so we had to share her not only with Ken, but also with his family. His mom, Crystal Abernathy, lived far enough away that Taylor and Ken had to do Christmas Eve with one family and Christmas Day with the other. We got Christmas Eve. David, Emily, and Isabel made us the Christmas Eve family too, and Aunt Jacquie and Nick came and brought Gran with them. Today, Christmas Day, would be much quieter. I tried not to feel sad about that.

This year's other change was that I had to get up

and out, holiday or not, to check on the dude ranch. Rising at six in the morning was now second nature. Though I never would have believed it possible, sometimes I woke up before my alarm.

Usually, when I got up to get ready for work, Dad was just pulling out of the driveway for his day at the factory and Mom was having a cup of coffee while she cleaned up his breakfast dishes and put food in the slow cooker for dinner.

But not on Christmas Day. The big house was more silent than I remembered it ever being. I grabbed clothes and crept down the stairs in my flannel pjs and robe. I would shower in the downstairs bathroom so I wouldn't wake up Ben, who was on Pacific Time, or Mom and Dad.

I stopped in the kitchen and turned on the coffeemaker. Surely, the others would be up before long, and I didn't want to face the horses without caffeine. My shower was quick, and I traded my pjs and slippers for heavy jeans, wool blend socks, and a thermal shirt with a long-sleeve button-up over it. The coffee was done, and I poured a travel mug full, added plenty of sugar and milk, and pulled on my new barn coat.

The coat was a gift from Ben that he'd arranged to ship from the retailer, and Mom wrapped it when it arrived. I'd been very excited to open it last night. Even one Christmas ago, a flannel-lined, cotton canvas barn coat would have been a lousy joke, but now it was perfect. The one I'd bought at the consignment shop wasn't holding up, and I needed a replacement. Assuming I stayed at the ranch for a while, which was more up in the air than ever.

The thermal-lined leather gloves Michael had given me were on the bench by the back door, and I slid them on after my lined rubber boots. Outside in the thin morning light, I started the car and headed toward the ranch with the radio playing Christmas music. The roads, predictably, were empty. Everyone in the Serendipity area was at their designated holiday destination or would be leaving for it at a more civilized time.

Taylor would awaken sometime this morning, in a bed next to her husband. The Abernathy family hosted a champagne brunch for friends, and late in the afternoon, a dinner that featured foods like clam chowder, oven-roasted vegetables with lobster, and a flaming dessert I forgot the name of. My brother-in-law and sister had talked about it last night and were both looking forward to it.

I had never spent a major holiday without my twin. That the first time was Christmas Day really sucked. We knew it would eventually happen, and we'd be fine. But it still hurt.

Next year, who knew? Ben seemed serious about his girlfriend out west. *Very* serious. Would he even be with us next year? Or would he have to choose between families too? In his case, we were talking real distance, so it might be Thanksgiving or New Year's with us, and Christmas with what's-her-name and her relations.

Someone started to croon *Have Yourself a Merry Little Christmas*, and I shut off the radio.

Thanks for the reminder that I'm doing exactly the opposite.

I didn't much like change unless it was my idea.

Go to college—good. Graduate with a degree I thought I'd enjoy using—good. Get stuck in a local job—not good. Lose that job—worse. Sign on at the Rocking H—good when I thought it would get me close to Jacob and bad when Jacob wasn't interested. Now, when I realized I had fallen for Michael, and Michael, though pleasant enough, was unattainable and out of my league on a variety of levels, so much worse.

I had to come to grips with the fact that I couldn't have him. My life was forever changed, now that I had experienced real love, albeit one-sided, as opposed to the infatuation I'd felt for Jacob. Romantic songs were either sad or heartbreaking. Seeing happy couples made me want to weep.

And Christmas. Christmas was suddenly a reminder of all the happiness I'd experienced over the years and never appreciated. The family holidays I'd taken for granted were fading like a skiff of snow on a sunny day.

I pulled into the ranch drive and up to the main building, slurped the last of my coffee, and stepped out into the cold day. I would do my walk-through to be sure no pipes had burst or any other calamity had occurred.

Everything in the low, long building was in perfect order, as it had been left and as it had been yesterday when I checked. Still, I took a bit longer than necessary because I was procrastinating about my next task.

I gave myself a pep talk as I walked across the yard to the barn.

You offered to watch the place so your friends could have a worry-free holiday. Cleaning the stalls is nothing you haven't done before and will mean less work when they get home. Sure, there is poop and lots of it, but you know a shower and load of laundry takes care of that. Plus, Dad's famous French toast will be waiting when you get home.

Dad cooking on Christmas morning was a tradition, and he promised to wait until I got home from my chores. He had no idea how much I was looking forward to it this year, because it meant I had mucked out the stalls by myself for the first time. I'd never *earned* French toast before, but this year I sure would.

The first step was to let the horses out into the paddock. They seemed glad to see me, probably realizing I was their ticket outdoors for some exercise.

I started with the gentlest mare. I pulled off one of my gloves and stuck it into a jacket pocket. On a flat, outstretched hand, I offered her one of the peppermints I had loaded my pockets with. When she had slurped it up, I slid her bridle on and secured it. I gave her another peppermint, followed by clipping on a halter rope. She seemed slightly surprised that I was doing this, and maybe by the extra candy, but when I opened her gate she walked sedately beside me. I led her into the paddock, slipped her a third peppermint, unclicked the short, thick rope, and closed the gate between us.

After offering a short prayer of thanks, I squared my shoulders, and chose another horse that was easy to handle. Finally, the only one still in the barn was Killer. He and I sized each other up as I approached his stall.

The peppermint barely balanced on the shaking palm as I extended my hand toward him, holding my breath. Killer eyed me suspiciously and got the candy in one quick, wet movement.

"There. That wasn't so bad, huh?" I spoke calmly, trying to reassure both of us.

Killer tossed his head.

"You don't want to be the only one who has to endure extra time with poop in your stall. That wouldn't be any fun, right?" I smiled at him, ever so slowly reaching out my hand again to stroke him if he would let me.

He glared at me, nostrils flaring, but didn't move.

I'm not sure which of us was more surprised when I touched his silky neck. He didn't flinch and I didn't pass out, though at this point I wasn't sure if I was breathing. His eyes didn't look wild anymore. Instead, he stepped right up to the gate and put his head over it, to give me better access. I was meant to be slipping on the bridle and lead rope, but instead stood there stroking his neck and face, gently scratching between his eyes as I'd seen Michael do.

He made a sound. Not the exasperated snort I was used to, but more of a moan. He rubbed his face along my shoulder and neck. I would be sporting a lovely patch of horse slobber after this interaction, but it was worth it.

"Aw. You miss Michael, don't you? I get it. That's why you were so mean when I first met you. And when Michael showed up here, you knew it was just temporary. That's an aggravation too. Poor Killer. Now that he's gone, you don't know how long it will be. So you're lonely, aren't you, sweetheart?"

A tear fell. I was almost sure it was mine.

I heard a footfall but thought it was one of the horses outside. When Michael spoke, Killer and I stepped apart from each other.

"Wow. That was impressive. Hannah, I didn't realize you're a horse psychiatrist." Smiling, he went to Killer and stroked his strong neck, spoke some soft words. The stallion rubbed his head on Michael, nuzzling gently.

I envied Killer the closeness and lack of restraint. I also felt like I was intruding on a private moment, then realized *I* was supposed to be here and Michael was *not*.

"Hey. Why aren't you in Florida with your

family? Did something go wrong?"

"Nothing bad. The family is together, and I had a great time but decided I needed to come back here."

My heart started to thump. Maybe he'd returned just to see me. But I didn't want to seem pathetic or make him feel bad. It wasn't Michael's fault I'd fallen in love with him. Or—not totally his fault.

I tried for a blasé tone. "Oh, so you're back alone? Did you leave something behind?"

"Yes, I'm alone. Flew in this morning. I was lucky to get a flight into Louisville and a rental car. My SUV is in Florida with the family."

Whether Michael knew it or not, he was torturing me by drawing this out. "Well, I'm glad you made it back. *For whatever reason.*" Hint, hint.

He slid on the bridle, attached the halter rope, and opened the stall gate. "Let me put Killer into the paddock with the others. Then you and I can talk."

I walked beside him, hurrying to keep up with his long strides. "I'm here to clean out the stalls."

Michael glanced down at me. "I'm surprised they left you that task to do alone. Would you rather muck out stalls than have a cup of coffee with me?"

"Of course not. And no one asked me to do it. I just thought…"

He shook his head, smiling. "You wanted to surprise us. Very nice. You've grown up in the short time I've known you, Hannah."

"I am *completely* grown up."

He sighed but didn't say anything further.

Killer entered the paddock, and Michael secured the latch. When the horse didn't move away, Michael scratched him between the eyes again. "Go on, boy. We'll have a run together in a little while." The horse seemed to understand. He tossed his head as if to nod and trotted off.

Michael faced me, his eyes hot and his smile strained. "Now for that coffee."

****

He made the coffee while I paced the kitchen. I didn't want to get my hopes up about this conversation or his reason for showing up here unexpectedly. When he had poured mugs of the steaming brew and set them on the chuck wagon table, he motioned to the chair across from him. "Please. Before you wear a path in the floor."

I was too anxious to relax but dropped into the chair and nearly scalded my mouth with the first sip. Setting the mug down again, I forced myself to wait until he explained what was going on. I didn't want coffee. I wanted to understand. No matter what Michael's reason was for being here—even if it had nothing to do with me—I needed to know.

I had muddled around for too long already, first thinking I was in love with his brother and then with him. Maybe what I really needed was to find a cheap place to live and a job of any sort far away from here. I'd hate to leave my family, though the idea had never bothered me in all the years Taylor and I talked about our futures. The fact that Taylor was married and settled here was only part of the reason for my mixed feelings.

Now that I was an official adult with a job and responsibilities, I felt differently about the old hometown. It wasn't as bad as I had always thought. In fact, it had real potential. Unique businesses like the Rocking H, Barbeque Basement, Once Upon a Time, and the tiny cabin B&B on the Standish tree farm were bringing visitors in. There was talk of a bookstore opening on the square, and the local theater group hoped to buy and renovate the old abandoned movie theater building on South Main. If I left now, I'd miss the possible rebirth of Serendipity, and I didn't want to miss it. I wanted to be a part of it.

Michael Hollingsworth notwithstanding.

Watching me, he sipped his coffee, and smiled. "So many thoughts passing through your mind. Care to share any of them with me?"

I sat back, trying to be comfortable in the chair and at ease with the situation. "We came in here for coffee so you could tell me something, Michael. My mind is just busy with *what ifs* that may or may not concern you."

He tipped his head, focused on my eyes. "I hope they do concern me. I hope that more than you can imagine." He expelled a long breath. "Okay, Hannah, I'll give it to you straight and simple. I'm not one for flowery speeches. I'm here because it's Christmas. I'm crazy about my family, but I couldn't imagine not spending at least part of Christmas with you."

My heart skipped a beat. "You ditched your family to see me?"

"I didn't permanently ditch them. You make me sound callous, and maybe I've given you reason to think that I am. But I'm not. I hugged and kissed them all—didn't kiss Jacob, I'll leave that to Christy who seemed more than glad to do so. I gave them each a gift, told them I had something important to do. When you live the kind of life I've become accustomed to, your family gets used to departures. You can't say hello again unless you say so long, you know."

"What? Let me get this straight. You came up here and scared me half to death on Christmas morning to tell me I need to say so long to my family?"

He laughed, shaking his head. "That's not my main message, but if you put that one in the back of your mind, we'll discuss it sometime. Maybe sometime soon, based on how fast Christy progresses.

"Hannah, I don't have much to offer. I don't

have a permanent address anywhere and prefer to decide on the spur of the moment which direction I'm headed next. You've seen a little bit of how I live. Drop in on the siblings, go visit the parents. For the most part, free of any burden except the occasional family request, like the one that brought me here."

I was grateful for that request. Should I eventually thank Christy for injuring herself so Jacob had to call in his brother to help at the ranch? No, that could never sound like a positive occurrence. Her career had ended with that accident. But—what if that was the only way she and Jacob could get back together? Would that, then, make it a good thing in Christy's mind?

My heart pounded. What was Michael saying exactly?

"Ever since I retired, this has been an ideal life. But now..." He searched my face which must have reflected my emotional confusion. "...I need more." Then his shoulders sagged. "Whatever you say, I'm good with it. I just needed to let you know."

I realized that, for the first time since I had met

him, Michael was flustered.

"Is there a question in there somewhere?" I asked, a hopeful smile pulling at the corners of my mouth.

He whooshed out a breath, his eyes rolling heavenward. "Maybe I left it out. I'm comfortable in a lot of situations, but this isn't one of them. Okay, I'll back up a little. Hannah, from the first time I met you at the Barbeque Basement, I haven't been able to get you out of my mind. No matter how much I tried to put distance between us, the only thing that's felt right is spending time with you. Even mucking out stalls together, I had a flash of what my future could be like if you were in it. Your enjoyment of life, willingness to wade into anything and do your best. A future with you in it would be so much better than anything I could have imagined before." He took a deep breath, reached across the table, and held both of my hands in his. "So here's the question. Hannah Kincaid, will you be my home base?"

"Like in baseball?"

He laughed, knowing I was teasing. "No. Like

in wherever you are, that's my home. If you live in Serendipity or if you get a job in New York City or somewhere in between. After a reasonable courtship, of course. Your family needs to be okay with me."

"And yours with me," I pointed out, trying to manage a calm tone while my heart was beating like a galloping stallion.

"You know my siblings are crazy about you, Hannah. Mom and Dad are eager for you to go down and visit. I think they're afraid you don't really exist. I might have made you sound too perfect."

I thought of the mistakes I'd made so far in my life. Assumptions I had made about my town, my family. Jacob. Michael. "Perfect is something I definitely am not."

He got up from the table and came over to me, pulled me to my feet, and touched his lips to mine. Our hearts were both racing, and the kiss became long and deep as we held each other in a tight embrace. A few minutes later, we drew slightly apart, gazing into each other's eyes.

"You don't have to be perfect in every way,

Hannah, to be perfect for me. And you nailed that without even trying."

It was wonderful to be loved for myself. When pursuing Jacob, I had struggled to change as much as necessary to become what he wanted. I knew that life with Michael would involve a steep learning curve, but I had proved to myself that difficult goals were achievable with enough hard work. And being a good partner for Michael was the best goal I could have because the feeling was mutual.

Heck, I had made friends with Killer. Nothing was impossible.

Epilogue

THE MAGIC THAT began that Christmas has continued in my life with Michael.

Christy's arrival altered the balance of life on the dude ranch for the better. Far from being a burden to any of us, she brought new vitality to the Rocking H. For the first few months her doctors forbade her to ride or do strenuous work, but any time the guests were in the chuck wagon, she was there too, ready to ask and answer questions or tell stories of her growing up in Montana and following the rodeo circuit.

The Hollingsworths figured into many of the adventurous tales of her youth. From the first moment I met her and saw her with Jacob, it was apparent how right he had been to wait for her. How many of us would have the fortitude and foresight to believe in first love and know it would survive years of living apart?

Sooner than expected, Christy and Jacob, Ashley, and Jessica didn't need extra help anymore. One Sunday afternoon in February, Michael and I were married by the stone fireplace in the chuck wagon, surrounded by family. We don't have a permanent address, nor plans to acquire one any time soon. Instead, we began our life together traveling and looking for ways to make a difference.

Far from being just that guy who retires and kicks back, Michael is in fact the guy who retires and does more than ever. We are seeing the world and learning about its people, while—we hope—helping others along the way.

Many of the world's people are living with daily concerns about basic necessities like food, clothing, and shelter. There are wells to be dug, water purification systems to be installed, and agricultural practices to improve in order to better use available resources. And so much more.

In ways I never expected, my environmental

management studies are continuing on a daily basis. Michael does, indeed, know people. At the time he made that statement, I assumed he was talking about finding me a start on the career ladder. But so much better than that, he helped me see how one person can make a difference to the environment and the people it supports. My expertise on the topic of fertilizer has come in handy many times.

Closer to home, we've developed a ten-acre field of wildflowers on the Rocking H. Turning the land over to native plants is aiding the honeybee population, which needs all the help it can get. Butterflies and hummingbirds love it too. Dude ranch guests can't get enough of the wildflower walk, a circuitous path mowed through the field of tall, multi-colored flowers that some might call weeds.

When the Serendipity mayor heard about and visited the wildflower walk, he asked us to develop something similar in a floodplain area of the town. For this project, which is several miles long and borders the two creeks that meander through the city limits, we had loads of help from townsfolks and school science classes.

Some tell us we've created a little bit of heaven in Serendipity. It might be more accurate to say we've let a little bit of heaven come back where it was a century or so ago. We've also developed strategies for other urban areas to do something similar.

Getting to know Michael has changed me in ways I would never have dreamed or even wanted to change. Maybe that's part of love. Growing together, day by day.

The End...
Or is it the beginning?

A Note from the Author

Thank you so much for taking the time to visit Serendipity, Indiana. I hope you enjoyed Hannah and Michael's story. It was fun to write!

Back when I wrote EMILY'S DREAMS, Hannah and Taylor were spoiled-rotten high school seniors. I'm so glad they grew up, fell in love, and instead of leaving Serendipity behind, have come to appreciate their family and their little hometown.

So many times we (myself included!) fail to see the beauty and unique opportunities that are right in our own back yard. Since I started this series, Serendipity has slowly begun the process of capitalizing on what makes it special. Maybe that's a lesson to put in our pockets—we don't have to become something *else* to be wonderful. We can just be the very best version of ourselves.

Happy reading!

Magdalena

For Free Reads, Sneak Previews & backstage info, become a Newsletter Subscriber!

I love to connect with readers! Please sign up for my newsletter so we can stay in touch. Don't worry about me clogging up your email inbox—I only send an email if I have actual news to share. The sign-up form is on my website. Just type into your browser: http://www.magdalenascott.com/p/contact.html

Also in the Serendipity, Indiana, series:

SMALL TOWN CHRISTMAS

Melissa is moving back to Serendipity, Indiana to raise her young son and run her new business—in spite of a painful past and the fact that her ex-boyfriend still lives in their hometown.

EMILY'S DREAMS

Emily Kincaid has a second chance at life, and a voice in her head that keeps nudging her along. But she can't move forward without dealing with her past.

CHRISTMAS WEDDING

Dec. 1: Jim Standish is ready—right this minute—to marry the love of his life, but Melissa Singer wants the day to be one they'll look back on forever. Planning and execution time: 25 days. Will it be possible to create the perfect Christmas Wedding?

THE BLANK BOOK

Alice Williams is surviving widowhood, but must unlock the secrets of a mysterious blank book before she can confidently step into her future with a man she's afraid to love.

THE RING

Happily-ever-after is out of the question. But in Serendipity, the Magic of Love does amazing things.

THE ROAD NOT TAKEN

Francie Standish Carrington has some tough decisions to make, and a lot of questions about a past she thought she understood.

A PIECE OF HER SOUL

Jacqueline needs a break from the constant strain of the special gift she has. But the little cottage on a quiet street isn't quite the retreat she expected, due to the presence of a handsome next door neighbor.

ONCE UPON A TIME

Taylor Kincaid has big plans for her life, and falling in love with the mysterious new shop owner in her hometown isn't one of them. Sweet romance, "coincidences" that might be more than that, and a love that survives the unthinkable come together in this new Serendipity, Indiana tale.

A COWBOY FOR CHRISTMAS

Hannah Kincaid has her eye on Jacob Hollingsworth, the handsome co-owner of Serendipity's new (and only) dude ranch. When Jacob's brother Michael shows up, everything at the Rocking H is turned on its head-- including Hannah's plans.

Magdalena's Legend, Tennessee Titles

MIDNIGHT IN LEGEND, TN

CHRISTMAS COLLISION

WHERE HER HEART IS

BUILDING A DREAM

SECOND CHANCES

CHRISTMAS CHARM

HOME FOR CHRISTMAS

UNDER THE MISTLETOE (Prequel)

THE HOLLY AND THE IVY (Prequel)

Kim: Beach Brides

Have you read all of the Serendipity, Indiana books, and all of the McClains of Legend, Tennessee titles? Maybe you'll enjoy KIM, a Serendipity-Legend mashup!

Twelve friends from the online group, Romantic Hearts Book Club, decide to finally meet in person during a destination Caribbean vacation to beautiful Enchanted Island. While of different ages and stages in life, these ladies have two things in common: 1) they are diehard romantics, and 2) they've been let down by love. As a wildly silly dare during her last night on the island, each heroine decides to stuff a note in a bottle addressed to her "dream hero" and cast it out to sea!

Almost two years later...

Jon Whitfield "landed" the message in a bottle on a fishing vacation with his buddies, and it disappeared before he could decide whether to respond. Now he's on a road trip with Kim Rose, whose gratitude in spite of a painful past reminds him of the touching note he wishes he'd kept.

The Beach Brides Series has 12 titles. Each book begins with the same premise, but is a stand-alone story with a happy-ever-after ending.

Kim—Prologue

Kim's message in a bottle...

I'm writing this letter under protest, because a bunch of my friends are each writing one. And no, I don't need to hear the old question, "If your friends were jumping off a cliff, would you jump too?"

Answer: No. But I would write this silly letter.

FYI—I don't expect this bottle to be found by the man of my dreams. Though I've had some rocky times, I am not *desperate for romance.*

I have a great career, friends, and a life I enjoy. I'm considering adopting a pet. So, you can see, when you read this sometime in the future, I'll probably be much too busy and happy to become involved with you.

This is just fair warning, because I am an extremely honest person. If you are married, please burn or shred this note. Or you can seal it back in the bottle and chuck it into the ocean again, if you're the romantic type.

If you are not married or in a relationship, and want to be my email pen pal, I might be open to that. But nothing more. I expect we have zero in common beyond a possible scientific curiosity, re: bottle floating from where I tossed it to wherever you found it.

Makes me think, for some reason, of Star Wars. *Are you a fan of sci fi?*

Do you believe people are fated to certain experiences?

And do you believe it's important to stand by someone even when leaving is immeasurably easier? If your answer to this question is "no," please forget this bottle came into your life.

Yours truly (because how else should I close this?)

whitecapkr@...

P.S. The girls are watching to make sure I fill up the page. Otherwise I would have written less.

Like this:

Hi. I don't believe you're out there.

Kim—Chapter One

THE PATIO OF Tony's Macaroni in Serendipity, Indiana was busy tonight. Kim Rose sipped her red wine, letting it slide down her throat as she anticipated a delicious meal. The weather was perfect. A warm breeze teased her with the rich, spicy smell of the neighboring table's lasagna. She glanced at a couple nearby, who seemed to be in a romantic world of their own.

When a car horn honked, her friend, Emily Standish, sitting across the table from her, raised a hand and waved.

A puff of wind blew some hair into Kim's eyes. She pulled an elastic out of her handbag and jerked her hair into a ponytail, hoping all of it would stay under control for once.

"Emily, do you know who that was? Or did you just wave *in case* you knew?"

Emily laughed. "Her name is Lauren. One of her sisters was in my high school graduating class."

Kim shook her head in amazement. "I'm not sure I'll ever get used to living in a small town. You seem to have a connection to everyone in Serendipity."

Emily leaned back in her chair, smiling. "That's one result of living in the same place all my life. But, Kim, you know more people every day." Emily tipped her head, concerned. "I hope you're not second-guessing your decision to move here."

Kim put a hand over her friend's. "Not second-guessing. I'm still in the adjustment period." For years, Kim had lived and worked in a vibrant community minutes away from the culture, shopping, and dining opportunities of Louisville, Kentucky. Except for the incredible speed of the gossip tree, everything in Serendipity moved at a slower pace than she was accustomed to. "Serendipity has a very different lifestyle. I'm learning how it works."

Emily nodded. "Remember, when I told you

that Serendipity Hospital was looking for nurses, I warned you of what to expect here."

"Yes, ma'am, I remember, and I told you I was ready for a drastic change. I love Serendipity. I feel happier than I have in a long time." She sipped more wine, to shut herself up and avoid getting maudlin about the past. "I'll have to be okay with the possibility that I'll never know as many people as you do. Sometimes I think you can call every one of the six thousand citizens by name."

Emily cringed. "In my sordid past, I probably called a few of them some names I shouldn't have. Good thing you dragged me down the road to recovery after my car wreck, and helped me change my attitude." She shook her head in dismay. "Sometimes I can't believe how rotten I was back in the day."

Kim laughed, glad for the change in subject. Before becoming a nurse, she had worked as an aid in the facility where Emily was sent for physical therapy and rehabilitation. At first, nobody wanted to be around the angry, bitter young woman. "You were certainly one of our most well-known patients."

Emily covered her eyes with her hands, shaking her head. Her words were muffled when she spoke. "Okay, I'm really wishing for some brain bleach here. Thank goodness I wasn't a lost cause."

"Nobody is a lost cause," Kim said. That belief was important to her sanity at work, and she had to believe it for herself.

Emily removed her hands, and leaned forward, elbows on the table. "Do you ever think about all the connections in our lives, things that happen and we don't realize the importance until later?"

Kim slowly twirled her wineglass on the table, wishing for the food to arrive, or for someone to recognize Emily and interrupt their conversation. *Anything.* "What kind of connections do you mean?"

Emily's eyes sparkled. "Well, my wreck for one. It was a terrible thing—for me, for my family. But so much good has come out of it."

Kim had a flash of Emily's wedding day. "Your relationship with David sure evolved during your rehab."

"Absolutely. He and I wouldn't have gotten

together otherwise. But so many things led up to that. And, Kim, getting to know you was a big life changer. You taught me a lot about gratitude, and about working hard to achieve a worthwhile goal."

Kim laughed. "I did? Really, I was just trying to keep you from giving up on yourself."

Her friend shook a finger at her. "Don't shrug it off, Kim. I'm serious. Your attitude toward life, after losing your mom to breast cancer, and going through that yourself—and the boyfriend who dumped you—"

Kim slid down in her chair, and whispered, "You're making me feel pretty awesome right now."

Emily frowned. "I don't mean to be negative. I'm talking about being grateful every day even when life is hard. That's what you taught me, Kim."

I'd love an instant re-play of those lessons. The audio version so I can listen on my phone whenever I need a lift.

Kim cleared her throat. "New topic. The road trip. Are you one hundred percent sure you can't go?"

An unusual look passed quickly over Emily's face. "Yes. One hundred percent. I'd love to see that area, and I will someday. But I want to make it a family vacation. Something David and I do together, and take Isabel when she's old enough to enjoy it. I know you're eager to go, and you're just being kind."

"Well, I am looking forward to it, but I'd step aside and let you go. I wouldn't know Travis and Suzanne without you introducing me. If you were up for it, we could both go. Surely there's room in their car for four. Not sure about four plus a car seat." She chuckled at her own joke.

Emily coughed, seemed to narrowly avoid spitting wine. "Oops. Excuse me—wine went down the wrong way."

She replaced her glass on the table, just as Tony, the restaurant co-owner, appeared with their hand-made pizza. It was beautiful, and smelled heavenly.

He set it on the table with a flourish. "You ladies need anything else right now?"

Emily looked at Kim and answered for both of them. "We're good, Tony. Thanks. It's a perfect night to eat on the patio. I'm so glad you added this."

He shook his head, chuckling. "Thanks. It hurts

to admit that it was the wife's idea, and I kept telling her nobody'd be interested. I'll be eating crow about that for the rest of my life, I guess."

"If you get to do that on the patio, it won't be so bad," Emily said.

Tony covered his ears, laughing. "Yeah, yeah, yeah." He excused himself and checked in with another table.

Emily served a slice of pizza to Kim, and put one on her own plate. "Back to the road trip. It's all yours, Kim. Have a great time, take loads of photos, and text them to me. I know you're ready for a break. You haven't taken a real vacation since that island trip with your book club friends, right?"

Kim chewed slowly, picturing scenes from Enchanted Island. "Yes. It's almost two years. We were chatting about it online the other night. Hard to believe."

And even harder to believe that some of the girls had actually met the men of their dreams through that ridiculous bottle toss. She hadn't told anybody outside the group about the message in a bottle. Not even Emily. She would probably have a good laugh about it if she heard, and Kim wasn't ready to provide that comic relief.

Kim was realistic. She didn't expect a knight in shining armor to sweep her onto his galloping white steed, and carry her off to live in a castle. She had to do the best she could with the life she had, and that meant learning, again, to be grateful each day. And being satisfied with experiencing romance by reading about it in novels. The real-life kind was too painful to risk again.

Gratitude changes lives, she'd heard. Evidently she'd said it a few times, and Emily had paid attention. Maybe it was time Kim re-learned the lessons she had taught her friend.

Nobody is a lost cause. Not even me.

Find KIM here:

http://www.magdalenascott.com/p/kim.html